Between Teens

Sarah Massry

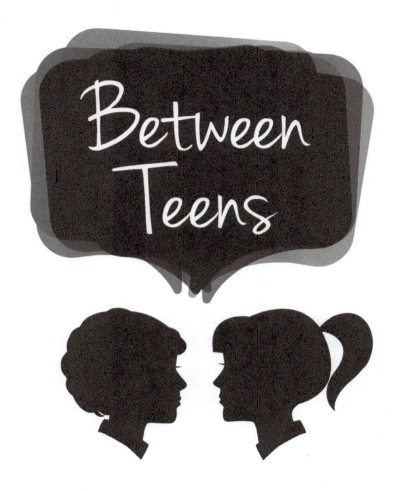

Between Teens

Sarah Massry

ISRAEL BOOKSHOP
Publications

Copyright © 2015 by Israel Bookshop Publications

ISBN 978-1-60091-362-4

Book design by: Rivkah Lewis

Published by:
Israel Bookshop Publications
501 Prospect Street
Lakewood, NJ 08701

Tel: (732) 901-3009
Fax: (732) 901-4012
www.israelbookshoppublications.com
info@israelbookshoppublications.com

Printed in the United States of America

Distributed in Israel by:
Shanky's
Petach Tikva 16
Jerusalem
972-2-538-6936

Distributed in Europe by:
Lehmanns
Unit E Viking Industrial Park
Rolling Mill Road,
Jarrow , Tyne & Wear NE32 3DP
44-191-406-0842

Distributed in Australia by:
Gold's Book and Gift Company
3- 13 William Street
Balaclava 3183
613-9527-8775

Distributed in South Africa by:
Kollel Bookshop
Ivy Common
107 William Road, Norwood
Johannesburg 2192
27-11-728-1822

Contents

Acknowledgments

First and foremost, I would like to thank the *Ribono Shel Olam* for all that He has done for me and for my family.

To my dear parents, Mr. and Mrs. Aaron and Nechama Pascal: Thank you for your constant love and guidance; thank you for believing in everything I do. Thank you to my in-laws, Mr. and Mrs. Charles and Ziza Massry, for your support and care and for everything you do for us.

To my sister, Chaya Kramer: Thank you for everything—and for coaching me from day one. To my dear sisters, Miriam and Devorah; to my sisters-in-law, Freidy, Chevy, Julie, Sarah, Ester, Oura, Shani, Kelly; and to my nieces, Judy and Aliza: You are truly the best. Thank you for your fabulous ideas and feedback.

To my dear high school friends, Brocha, Chani, Chanie, Esty, Gitty, Henny, Nechama, Rivka, and Shaindy: Thank you for the wonderful teen memories. I treasure our friendships.

My heartfelt thanks to *Mishpacha TeenPages* and *Ami Magazine,* where some of the stories in this book first appeared. To the brilliant and talented editors that I have the privilege of working with, Rechy Frankfurter, Yitta Halberstam Mandelbaum, Sarah Rivka Kohn, Avigail Sharer, and Daniela Thaler: Thank you for your constant encouragement.

To M.C. Millman: Thank you for inspiring me to write.

To the staff of Israel Bookshop: Working with you has been a pleasure. Mrs. Malkie Gendelman—thank you for your expert editing job. Mrs. Leah Gruskin and Mrs. E.M. Sonenblick—thank you for the thorough proofreading you gave this book. Mrs. Rivkah Lewis—thank you for the excellent typesetting job and the beautiful cover design.

Finally, thank you to my dear family, my husband Ezra and precious daughter Aliza, for your constant support and contributions to my work.

Sarah Massry

SECTION 1

School Days

The Measure of My Worth

Was she serious? Had Malky just said that she loved finals? "I'm sorry, Malky, I think I'm not hearing right. Did you just say that you love *finals*?" I asked her.

Malky giggled lightly. "No, you're not hearing things. That's *exactly* what I said!"

I gave her a confused look. "Oh, I know what you mean," I finally said. "After the three weeks of finals, school is over! That's why you're excited."

"Nah, I actually mean that I *like* finals. It's a nice change of routine. No classes, school starts late, we take two finals, and we're out of there!"

"Yeah," added Dina. "Then we can hang out and party for the rest of the day!"

I couldn't believe it. They were missing an integral

component here. "Um, hello," I interjected, "have you forgotten something? In between the 'partying,' we have some murderous finals to study for and take!"

They shared a laugh. "Yeah, well, how long does it take to study already?" asked Malky. "I mean, there *are* twenty-four hours in the day…"

Dina shared her "finals plans," which included shopping in the city. Malky couldn't wait to go swimming and also hoped to get some camp shopping done.

Personally, I planned to study, and do nothing else. The conversation was so frustrating to me that I simply walked away.

Malky's words reverberated in my mind. *How long does it take to study already? I mean, there are twenty-four hours in the day…*

How long does it take *me* to study? Let's just put it this way…I hoped that the twenty-four hours in the day would suffice!

When our finals schedules were handed out, I felt sick to my stomach. I just didn't get it. How were we supposed to study for—and then take—*two* finals in one day?! Was that humanly possible?

My eyes scanned the chart. Hmm…the first day was *Navi* and *Dikduk*. All I could think was: *Help!*

When the bell rang, I gathered my things and walked briskly out of the building, hoping that the fresh air would calm me down.

I ran into Malky. "Hey, Batya," she said, "isn't it a gorgeous day? I just love this weather! I can't wait; we're opening our pool next week!"

"Um, yeah, it's pretty nice out," I said in a distracted

voice. Then I mumbled some sort of goodbye and made my escape. I felt like I needed to be alone.

It actually was a glorious day. The sky was a brilliant blue, the sun was strong, and there was a gentle breeze in the air. But I couldn't focus on any of that; all I could think about was the terrifying finals schedule we had just received.

Schoolwork had always been a challenge for me. I had never received top grades in elementary school, but I had always managed, somehow or other, to pull through. It wasn't exactly a walk in the park, but with the help of my tutors and a slightly modified curriculum, I'd been able to pass my tests and graduate to the next grade each year. But high school was a lot more difficult than elementary school. So far, I was holding up...but only by the skin of my teeth. Now it was finals time, and everyone knows how hard high school finals are. I felt like I was doomed.

Well, finals began, and however difficult I thought they would be, they were so much harder. Monday was *Navi* and *Dikduk*. I spent the entire Sunday studying *Navi*, literally from 9:00 a.m. until 7:00 p.m. I hardly even stopped to eat. By 8:00 p.m. I felt restless. I couldn't sit any longer.

"Hey, why don't you go for a walk or something?" suggested my older sister. "It's good to air out."

I was tempted to do just that, but I knew I couldn't afford the time. I had not even begun studying for my *Dikduk* final yet, and it was already eight o'clock at night!

I began to panic.

I tried to calm down enough to actually study. I pulled out my notes, but found it hard to concentrate.

Next, I called my friend, Dina. Perhaps she could help me out. But I had no such luck. She couldn't help me because she was on her way home from the mall.

Frustration rose up within me. Dina was partying at the mall, while I was having the most miserable, excruciatingly difficult time of my life! The pure injustice of it all!

Finally, feeling that I had reached my wits' end, I decided to call Miriam, my tutor from the previous year, and ask for help.

When I entered high school, I had thought that I'd outgrown my tutor. I felt like I would be able to manage on my own. Most girls in high school do not have tutors, and I so badly wanted to fit in. I thought I could always ask my friends and classmates for a bit of extra help or clarification when needed. But apparently, as I was now realizing, I couldn't manage on my own. The pressure was really getting to me.

I apologized to Miriam for the last-minute notice, explaining the urgency of the matter. She must have heard the quavering of my voice, the humiliation of being forced to ask for help, and she immediately agreed to come over and study with me.

We studied for a solid two hours, yet I still felt hazy about the material.

"With *Dikduk,* you really have to practice," she advised me on her way out. "Otherwise, it is hard to retain the material."

I felt hot tears sting my eyes. Practice? When was I supposed to practice? It was already ten o'clock at night, and I had been studying since early that morning!

I tried to practice my conjugations, but by eleven

o'clock my eyes were drooping. I finally gave in to them and crawled into my bed—but not before setting the alarm clock for 5:00 a.m. If I couldn't finish studying now, I'd have to finish in the morning.

Monday was one of the longest days of my life. I dragged myself out of bed at 5:16 a.m. (after hitting the snooze button twice) and made an attempt at *Dikduk* practice. By the time I caught the bus to school, I already had a headache. The *Navi* final was okay; I felt pretty confident about it. But the *Dikduk* final was not okay. *Dikduk* had never been my strong point, and I stared helplessly at the test paper. I did my best to write down as many coherent answers as I could.

At one point, I noticed that the girls in my class had started to hand in their papers.

"That wasn't too bad," said Dina on her way out of the room.

How dare she say that! I thought, clutching my pen. *Especially after she spent the day at the mall yesterday, while I slaved over my books!* I scanned my own test paper. *There is no way I'm going to pass*, I suddenly realized. I had to control my tears. *Don't cry!* I commanded myself. *I am a high school girl!*

The rest of finals passed in a miserable, difficult, and sleepless blur. Three weeks later, I was finally able to take a deep sigh of relief—finals were over! It was summer! I was set to spend my summer as a counselor in a local day camp, and I was really looking forward to it. I love kids, especially six-year-old girls, and that was to be the age of the girls in my bunk.

On the last day of school, we were required to attend an end-of-the-year assembly, after which our report cards would be distributed. I honestly can't recall much about what happened at the assembly; I was far too nervous about receiving my report card. The principal spoke for a very *loooong* time. Then, the G.O. performed some sort of funny skit and gave out some prizes. It seemed like everyone else was having a grand time, but not me. Not with the thought of what was coming afterwards.

At long last, I received the manila envelope which contained my report cards. My hands were shaking slightly as I opened it. I glanced through the English one first. I smiled. I had passed everything! I had even done pretty well in a couple of subjects! Then I pulled out the Hebrew report card. A quick scan revealed that I had passed everything...aside from *Dikduk*.

I made a mad dash for the door, hoping to get out of the school building as quickly as possible.

No such luck. Malky caught up with me. "Hey, didn't do so well?" she asked. I guess my facial expression gave that away. She put her arm around me. "It doesn't matter! It's not your marks that get you far in life. You're still a great person."

Easy for you to say! I wanted to shoot back. Although she was trying to be kind, her words made me feel even worse.

Thankfully, I had no time to harp on my failing *Dikduk* grade. Camp was to begin two days later, and there was work to do: a bunk room to set up, charts to create, and parents to call. The girls in my bunk were a lovely bunch and simply adorable. As camp progressed and we settled into a routine, I found myself enjoying the sunny days with "my girls." I took them swimming, we made projects together, and played games and sang songs. I was in my element, and I could tell that my campers loved every minute, too.

Two weeks into the summer, Mrs. Taub, the mother of one of my campers, walked into our bunk room.

"Are you the famous Morah Batya?" she asked with a wide grin.

"Yes, I am!" I beamed.

"I'm *thrilled* to meet you!" she gushed. "I had to drop something off at the camp office this morning, and I was so excited to have the chance to finally meet you. My Rikki has not stopped talking about you since the first day of camp! She adores you to pieces! She even plays 'Morah Batya' and pretends to be you! Thank you for giving her the best summer of her life!"

As she walked away, I looked over at Rikki and gave her a warm smile. She smiled back. It was true that Rikki loved me. In fact, so did the rest of my bunk. *Baruch Hashem,* we were all getting along so well and having a wonderful summer together. I had even overheard some of my girls saying that I was the "best, nicest, and funnest" counselor in the world. *Bet these kids don't realize that I failed my* Dikduk *final!* I thought with a wry grin.

But then it hit me. It really didn't matter. Because my *Dikduk* grade did not define me as a person, nor did it measure what I am worth. I could be a successful person regardless of the grades I achieved in school.

I had always heard about the people who failed at school and then went on to succeed in life. In fact, I'd heard that Thomas Edison, one of the most brilliant inventors of all time, never even made it through high school! Yet these stories were always so difficult for me—a student whose entire life seemed to center around grades—to comprehend. I mean, let's be real: Wasn't a high school girl's life all about the marks she received?

But at last, in the blissful months of this summer, I was able to step back and view myself as a person, not just as a student. I was able to see that yes, school was not "my thing," but that there was so much more to me than my report card and grades. I could still be a top-notch counselor. I could still be a successful person. I could still go far and achieve great things in life.

Organizationally Challenged

It was towards the end of eleventh grade when I was approached by a classmate of mine. "Dini, I was absent yesterday. Can I borrow your Chumash notes, please?"

"Sure," I answered. This was quite a routine request for a high school girl. I slipped my loose-leaf out of my schoolbag, flipped open to the Chumash section, and took out the pages that she needed.

"Wow, thanks a ton," she said. "For some reason, I had trouble tracking down yesterday's lesson. But you are so organized! It's such a pleasure!"

I smiled to myself. *You are so organized.* Those words echoed in my mind. Ha! If only she knew the truth. The day was almost over, and as I walked home from school that afternoon, I felt my mind drifting down memory lane, to the very beginning of high school...

In elementary school, I was the most disorganized kid in the class. You know the type of girl who never has the right book at her desk, is forever losing her worksheets, and is always borrowing pens and papers from her classmates? Well, that was me.

Of course, I didn't *want* to be that way. I'd start off the year with my briefcase neatly packed with all the required school supplies, and I had every intention of keeping it that way. But my briefcase never remained in that pristine state for very long. Or, to put it more precisely, it hardly lasted a day.

See, it really wasn't my fault! The teachers would start handing out papers by the dozen (at least it *felt* that way!). There were schedules, worksheets, songs, letters to the parents, sheets that were meant to serve as covers to notebooks, and more schedules... I used to think that my teachers held stock in the paper companies! Well, in any case, by the time the first week of school was over, all these lovely worksheets and papers were usually in a neat—or not so neat—pile at the bottom of my briefcase. On a good year, they'd be stuffed into a random folder or loose-leaf.

Did my habits frustrate my teachers? Of course they did! I practically never had my homework completed, and when a teacher would ask the class to pull out a worksheet, I'd have to sheepishly raise my hand and ask for another one. Or else I'd discreetly follow along with a girl beside me.

Then there was the food and beverages. Remember that stack of papers at the bottom of my briefcase? Well, if my Snapple or tuna sandwich sort of leaked onto it, it surely complicated things. So even if I technically did have the right sheet, I couldn't exactly pull it out in the state that it was in...

Oh, and as for my bedroom? That is a story for another time. Let's just say that finding my uniform sweater, shoes, and socks each morning was not as simple as it sounds. Neither was finding my bed at night.

Truth be told, I am a smart and capable girl. So, why couldn't I just snap out of my messy habits? Why couldn't I just get my life together? That is a good question. When the teachers would ask my class to open our loose-leafs to a specific page, I would look longingly at the girls around me. To make matters worse, I was somehow always seated near the most organized girls in the class, and I was able to witness the stark differences between us. As my neighboring classmates neatly slipped their papers out of the correctly labeled sections of their loose-leafs, I would make a mad scramble through the papers in my briefcase, hoping that my water bottle had been closed tightly enough that morning...

When it happened that I couldn't produce the right paper (that the rest of the girls so effortlessly pulled out), I would feel the frustration mount within me. I would feel anger, too, but it was directed at myself. Why couldn't I be like everyone else? I really wanted to change. I wanted to be super-organized. Even a little organized would be good enough. But old habits are hard to break. So could I ever shake off my terrible tendency to be disorganized? That was the million-dollar question.

Old habits *are* hard to break. No one can deny that!

But thankfully, I was very determined. And if there is a will, there is a way.

When I entered high school, I was presented with a fresh start. The teachers and most of the girls in my grade did not know me. They did not know about my old ways and tendencies—and I was determined to keep it that way!

The first day of ninth grade arrived. If I had thought that eighth graders received a lot of handouts, it was *nothing* compared to ninth graders! We had about a million teachers (okay, slight exaggeration), not to mention rule books. The *chessed* heads and G.O. heads even handed out some *more* papers—in case we didn't have enough! I was so overwhelmed from that first day, that organizing all the papers was the last thing on my mind. I was lucky to have managed to find a few seconds to stuff all the handouts into my schoolbag!

I came home from school exhausted, and only vaguely aware of my messy schoolbag. A tiny voice inside of me tried suggesting, "Dini, sit down and organize your papers before they pile up!" But I was tired and stressed and had zero patience, so I tried my best to ignore that annoying voice.

The second day of school arrived. There were more teachers, more papers, and more *stuff*. Of course, this included my lunch and snacks, too (school ended really late!), which joined the pile inside my schoolbag.

It was not until the bus ride home from school that the painful truth hit me: I was slipping back into my old, disorganized ways. Give it another day or two, or maybe a couple of weeks, and my disorganized reputation would come right back. I looked over at the girl sitting next to me and glanced into her loose-leaf.

"Wow, you have it all together," I mumbled, more to myself than to her.

At first she looked surprised, and then she shrugged. "Oh, you mean my loose-leaf? Nah, it's really not such a big deal. If I don't start off on the right foot, then forget about it!"

I slumped back into my seat. She was right. If she didn't start off on the right foot—then she would be like me! I certainly had not started off on the right foot. So I was a lost cause, wasn't I?

What a shame. What a terrible, awful shame. Here I was, only the second day of high school, and I had already blown it.

When I walked into my house that night, I was in a foul mood. I went straight to my bedroom. The clothing sprawled over my bed and floor and the other junk lying around my room only added to my misery.

I stuffed my schoolbag into my closet. I just couldn't face it. I crawled into bed.

It was all over. I was destined to remain a slob for the rest of my life. There was absolutely no hope for me. *Who ever said that old habits are hard to break?* I thought miserably to myself. *That person is wrong. Dead wrong. Old habits are not hard to break. They are impossible to break!*

Just then, my sister knocked on my door.

"What is it?" I asked, rather harshly.

"I just wanted to return something to you," she said, poking her head into my room. She handed me a hole puncher. "Remember you bought this at Staples the other day? I borrowed it but forgot to give it back to you."

I hastily took the hole puncher from her, realizing sheepishly that I hadn't even noticed it was gone. Because I hadn't even attempted to use it.

"Thanks a ton," my sister continued. "This thing is so easy to use! It can punch a whole stack of papers at once."

As soon as she walked out of my room, something stirred within me and I decided to try out the hole puncher myself. I pulled the stack of papers out of my schoolbag and hole-punched the entire thing. Then, I sat down and organized all the papers into my loose-leaf. Right then. I didn't stop until every last handout was in its proper place.

When I was done, well, it is hard for me to describe how I felt. Let me just say it felt great. I felt like I was finally in control.

Once I was in that new and transformational "organization mode," I decided to tackle my room, too. I put away all of my clothing and shoes and took all food products out of my room and back into the kitchen.

It was tedious work, but when I finished, I honestly felt like a new person. My room still wasn't perfect, but at least it looked like a civilized mess, not a disaster zone.

I wish I could end off by saying that from that day on, I turned into a super-organized person and lived a beautiful, mess-free life forever after. But that would be far from the truth. Because, as it turns out, old habits *are* hard to break. Not *impossible* to break, but certainly quite difficult to get rid of...

Difficult, though, is still doable. Throughout ninth

grade, I made a great attempt to stay on top of my things: my schoolbag, papers, books, and bedroom. I wasn't always perfect, but I did manage to stay pretty organized most of the time. At least I didn't acquire the awful reputation of "class slob" or "the messy student" (or to be more politically correct, and as one teacher once wrote on a report card, "organizationally challenged"). I was just a regular girl, who sometimes didn't have her papers, but usually did.

By tenth grade, it had become easier. My lazy and messy habits were no longer something I had to constantly battle. By eleventh grade, I finally had things down pat. I am glad I did, too, because at that age, I had already begun to dream of the future home I would hopefully build one day. I realized that if I hadn't learned to keep a schoolbag in order, the chances of my keeping a home neat and organized were almost non-existent.

Now, when people comment that I am an "organized person," I laugh to myself. If only they knew what I used to be like! This is precisely the reason why I share my story: to give hope to other "organizationally challenged" teens out there. I want to tell them all that old habits are *not* impossible to break, and that their dreams of conquering their messy streak *can* come true! Take it from me...

The Coffee Klatch

Coffee Klatch: A definition: An informal social gathering for coffee and conversation. It can also be defined as a social event where people have conversations about unimportant things.

There we were, sitting in the back of the classroom, partaking in our daily coffee klatch (a.k.a. history class). Aside from the coffee (we were actually sipping water and diet Coke), we were following the above definition to a tee.

Was it a social gathering? For sure. Were we discussing unimportant things? To be precise, we were actually debating the virtues of various brands of shampoos. How's that for unimportant?

"You seriously wash your hair with Herbal Essences

shampoo?" Rochel Leah was asking in a hushed whisper. "It smells, like, so *flowery*." She scrunched her nose. "I *so* do not like it!" I sat up straight, prepared to argue back. I *loved* my Herbal Essences shampoo!

But just then, Mrs. Krieger, our history teacher up in the front of the classroom, turned in our direction. She shot us a disapproving glare and shook her head before continuing on with her lesson. This caused me to pause—for almost ten seconds—before letting Rochel Leah know that, "You are *so* wrong. Herbal Essences is *great*; my hair comes out so sleek with it."

And so the conversation continued. One thing led to another, and within minutes, Rochel Leah was talking about her sister's upcoming wedding. Never mind the fact that we had already discussed this topic ad nauseam. Here we were, at it again.

There was a slow and steady drizzle outside our classroom window. I glanced at my watch. There was still another half hour until the bell.

I looked over at Rochel Leah, who was now sketching a rough version of her gown. Unfortunately, she is not artistically inclined, so her drawing looked more like a stick figure than a glamorous gown. Yawn. I glanced up at my teacher, who was talking about some war that happened at some time. Double yawn.

I turned back to Rochel Leah. "So, what color is your gown again?"

Rochel Leah tapped her pen on the drawing. "Hello? Which planet do you live on? My gown is champagne—you know that!"

"Oh, right! You've mentioned it before!"

At that moment, Mrs. Krieger called my name. "See

me after class," she requested in a somber tone.

That silenced the class.

I nodded and turned back to my notebook. I couldn't believe it! All I wanted to do after class was dash home. Now, I'd be forced to stick around for a lecture from my history teacher.

I slumped miserably in my seat. The whole thing was so terribly unfair! I mean, some of the others—like Rochel Leah—had been disrupting the class far more than I had. Again, I snuck a glance at my watch. But I was no longer counting down the minutes until the bell.

When the class emptied out of the room, I walked slowly to the teacher's desk.

"I'm so sorry for talking in class," I began, thinking that if I apologized right away, maybe I'd be able to get out of there faster.

"Your disruptive behavior is completely unacceptable," Mrs. Krieger said. "Aside from the outright chutzpah and disrespect, you are preventing other girls from participating in the lessons."

I nodded slowly. It was on the tip of my tongue to protest that there were girls who were even more disruptive than me. But I felt like it was smarter to remain silent, so I did.

"Do you realize that there is a history exam at the end of the week?" Mrs. Krieger questioned.

I nodded.

"And that there is a state test at the end of the year?" she persisted.

I nodded again.

After talking sternly for another few minutes, Mrs. Krieger finally let me go. I apologized once again and dashed out of the classroom as quickly as I could. I thought about the encounter for another few minutes, but by the time I got home, it had completely slipped my mind.

Later that evening, I spoke to Rochel Leah on the phone.

"By the way, what did Mrs. Krieger want from you after class?" she asked.

"Nothing much," I replied quickly, and then changed the topic. I didn't think it was nice of her to rub it in.

During history class the following day, I made a point of keeping my mouth shut. I even dragged my desk away from the "coffee klatch." (Though I did keep my desk close enough to keep tabs on the conversation—just in case the girls began talking about something interesting.)

As it turned out, I had no need to worry. The conversation that afternoon was as silly as ever. Mrs. Krieger taught. I doodled. The rest of the "coffee klatch" chatted.

When Mrs. Krieger mentioned the upcoming exam, a few of the girls in the "coffee klatch" suddenly sat upright in their seats and looked straight ahead. Rochel Leah began fumbling for notes, whispering loudly to the girl beside her.

"Girls, I need quiet, please," Mrs. Krieger called.

The whispering from our corner of the classroom dropped a notch or two. Another glare from Mrs. Krieger, and it quieted down completely.

When the bell rang a few minutes later, my friends and I all scrambled to try to get a hold of the best set of notes possible. Blimy's notes were okay. The problem was that she wrote down every single word the teacher said, including attendance! Aidel's notes were very neat, but not very clear. Hands down, Nechama had the best notes in the grade. We borrowed them for a couple of minutes and photocopied them in the office.

Next came the difficult part: studying for the actual exam. Mrs. Krieger's tests were known to be difficult, and I sighed as I perused my neat stack of stapled notes. There was so much material on the exam!

Sure, Nechama's notes were great. But great notes are still no substitute for a teacher, and unfortunately, I was basically teaching the material to myself for the first time ever. I crammed, studied, and I called a studious friend, who so kindly gave me a midnight crash course.

The following day, I spent my early morning and all the morning recesses painstakingly memorizing dates and names. By the time the history test rolled around, I actually felt confident about the material.

When Mrs. Krieger returned our test papers the next day, I smiled. I had thankfully received an excellent grade. A quick survey of the members of the "coffee klatch" confirmed that my friends had also received decent grades.

"Not bad for cramming all the material into one night of studying!" Rochel Leah proclaimed. The others giggled, but I was silent. I glanced up at Mrs. Krieger, who was trying to begin the new chapter. She wasn't having an easy time talking over the din of our voices.

I felt a pang. Something about the scene just did not feel right to me.

With my conscience bothering me, I resolved to improve in my class performance. I inched my desk away from my friends and took out a crisp piece of loose-leaf paper. I began taking copious notes. When Mrs. Krieger shushed the "coffee klatch" in the midst of her lesson, I mentally patted myself on the back. *Hey, for once she isn't talking to me,* I thought. *No guilty feelings or apologies necessary today!*

But after a few days, my resolve wore off. The Incas, the Egyptians, the pyramids...it was all so painfully boring! Also, the conversation beside me actually sounded quite exciting one afternoon. Rochel Leah had the rundown on the seniors' seminary choices. I began listening with half an ear. After all, I just had to know which seminary my choir head would be going to next year!

Then, when I had something to contribute to the conversation, I found that it was just too difficult to keep my mouth shut. So I offered my opinion to the "coffee klatch"...and whispered some comments...and cracked a few jokes...

I tried to justify my decision to talk in class. History was the last period of the day, and honestly, the school day was way too loooooong. I needed some time to relax. Everyone did, right? I was a star student during the other periods, so it didn't really matter if I talked just through Mrs. Krieger's class, did it? Anyway, all the other girls yapped through her lessons, so it wasn't like my occasional comments would make or break anything.

"Girls! I said quiet!" Mrs. Krieger disrupted my thoughts with her usual glare and sigh of despair.

After class, she informed us about another history exam. This time, though, I wasn't *that* nervous. The last test had gone rather smoothly, even without my listening during class. I wasn't terribly worried about the

Regents state test at the end of the year, either. I had actually heard about a fantastic crash course. One day of learning can make up for a whole year of classes! How amazing is that?

But by the end of the year, I was no longer so sure that taking a "fantastic crash course" instead of paying attention in class was all that amazing. Although I pulled off an excellent grade on my Regents history exam, I felt like I had failed. The niggling feelings of guilt that had been gnawing at me throughout the entire year finally got the better of me one day that summer, and I decided to call Mrs. Krieger at home.

"I am so sorry about the way I behaved during your classes," I told her.

Since she was quiet, I plowed on. "I feel really bad... I hope you can forgive me."

Mrs. Krieger was silent for a moment before she replied. "It was a very, very difficult year for me. I...I don't think I will be returning next year."

I felt so terrible that I wanted to cry. Had I caused Mrs. Krieger so much grief that she decided to quit teaching because of it? How had I allowed myself to behave in such a horrible way?

In the end, out of the goodness of her heart, Mrs. Krieger forgave me, and I hung up the phone feeling slightly better.

However, that phone call was one of the most difficult ones I ever had to make. True, it's hard to behave and keep quiet during a boring class. But it's even harder to ask forgiveness for a sin as grave as paining a teacher.

The Pursuit of Fun

Midwinter vacation: *Day Number One*
Shrill, shrill, shrill. My alarm clock persisted in making itself heard.

Already? I promptly ignored it and rolled back over. Vaguely, I heard it continuing to ring through my deep sleep, but I didn't care. I was tired. My peaceful slumber was interrupted by my younger sister.

"Could you please turn off that alarm clock already?" she bellowed. "It's vacation! I am trying to sleep!"

Did she say vacation? I shot up in bed. Right! It was vacation! I looked at my watch and gasped. It was 8:42 already! I quickly got dressed and, within minutes, I was standing in front of my mirror with a blow-dryer.

By now, my sister had had it. "Sarala," she said,

sitting up in her bed. "It's vacation! For once in my life I could actually sleep in! But first your alarm clock went off, and now this blow-dryer! *Puh-lease* can you let me sleep?"

"Yeah, sure," I mumbled. I craned my neck to see how the back of my hair looked. "As soon as I'm done, I'll be out of here."

My sister sighed heavily. "Forget it; my beauty sleep is ruined." She tossed back her hair and glared at me. "I don't understand you! Today is the day to chill and *relax*. Why are you up and about? Where exactly are you going?"

I laughed lightly. "I have places to go and people to meet! Personally, I don't plan on wasting my day in bed!"

"Sleeping late is not—"

I cut my sister off. "I plan on having fun today!" With that, I grabbed my camera and pocketbook and was off. As for my little sis? She was welcome to sleep away her midwinter vacation, if she so fancied. But not me, no siree. I had other plans.

Or at least I *thought* I had plans. My friends were supposed to be at my house at 9:00 a.m. sharp. We would go out for breakfast and then catch the 10:00 a.m. bus to the city. There, we'd meet up with our camp friends for the day.

I looked impatiently at my watch. It was already 9:05, and my friends were nowhere in sight.

I called Raizy. No answer. Next, I tried Leah, whose mother told me that she'd relay my message as soon as Leah woke up.

I gasped. Leah was still *sleeping*? How could she be!

At this rate, we'd miss the 10:00 a.m. bus and then our day would be ruined!

"Is everything okay, sweetheart?" asked my mother.

I gritted my teeth. "Yeah, I'm just running a bit late over here, and—"

"Late? But it's vacation!"

I was desperate to have a great time, and no one quite understood. With all the pressure of school, tests, and most recently midterms, I needed to have some real fun and unwind. What was wrong with that?

By the time my friends made it over to my house, it was 10:45 a.m. We had to skip breakfast in the bagel store, and instead munched on some whole wheat crackers as my mother quickly drove us to catch the 11:00 a.m. bus.

"Hey, cheer up, Sarala!" said Leah in an annoyingly bright voice. "It's vacation!"

"Don't remind me," I grumbled.

Leah just shrugged and then continued talking to Raizy. Sure, they were both in terrific moods, because they'd slept in. On vacation, no less. And because of that, while we were *supposed* to have been feasting on bagels, home fries, and orange juice, I was now trying to satiate my rumbling stomach with a bland cracker.

"Looks like there's traffic," I heard Raizy saying.

My heart sank. "Are you *serious*?" Sure enough, a quick glance out the window confirmed the horrid news.

Now our day was *doubly* ruined!

By the time we *finally* made it into the city, I was so tired of sitting, and so cranky, that I hardly enjoyed my day. Sure, I put on a smile (if you can call it that) and pretended to have fun, but inside, I was annoyed at the turn of events. I had been looking forward to my midwinter vacation for months. But now, when it came down to it, I was having a pretty lousy time.

Adding insult to injury, my mother served Shabbos leftovers for dinner that night, and I mistakenly became *fleishig*. So when my friends went out for ice cream that night, I had to settle with a Snapple.

But as I drifted off to sleep that night, I took comfort in the fact that tomorrow was another day. Day two of vacation. A brand-new day and a brand-new start. My mother had promised to take us to a faraway mall. Hopefully, it would be fun.

Midwinter vacation: Day Number Two

Learning from the previous day, I did not quite jump out of bed right away. I wasn't going to sit around, all dressed and bundled up in my coat, while the rest of the world caught up on their beauty sleep. So I took it easy.

But by 10:00 a.m., I was getting annoyed. It was really time to get going.

"Come on!" I pleaded with my sister. "Get up! Mommy said we can't leave until you're ready!"

"Soon!" the muffled reply emerged from my sister's pillow.

I threw my pillow at her. "The mall is closing soon! We'd better get going!"

"Yes, in about ten and a half hours!" My sister laughed. "There's no rush."

I shook my head. She *so* didn't get it. "Yeah, but it's far away! And I have other stuff to do when I get back!"

My sister grudgingly stumbled out of bed at 10:50 a.m. From the looks of it, you would have thought that she was waking up at the crack of dawn.

"I still don't understand why we have to get up so early," she said, rubbing her eyes.

"EARLY? It's halfway through the day!"

After a quick breakfast (again, no time for the bagel store), we were off to the mall. Thankfully, there was no traffic, and we made it to our destination in record time. I allowed myself to relax. Things were looking brighter.

We started off in a large department store, but I had no luck finding any clothes for myself. My mother and sister, though, found mountains of stuff to try on. With a yawn, I settled myself in a large armchair outside the dressing room, waiting for them to finish their try-ons.

"So, isn't it great that we got here so early?" My sister winked in my direction.

She did have a point. I do not particularly enjoy shopping. I never did. So why had I been so desperate to come here this morning? Well, because this mall was supposed to be fabulous, big, and fun.

To make a long story short, the mall was not fabulous *or* fun. But it sure was BIG, almost as big as the pounding headache I had as we walked back to our car. My vacation was getting worse by the day.

"Um, Ma?" I asked sheepishly, as she merged onto the highway. "I was thinking. Like, maybe we can stop and *do* something on the way home?"

My mother glanced into her rearview mirror. "But sweetheart, it was your idea to go to this mall in the first place! You said it would be fun!"

"Right, but, um..." My voice trailed off. You can't argue with logic. "Ah...I forgot that I hate shopping."

My sister dissolved into a fit of annoying giggles, and my mother tried her best to stifle her own amusement. "It's late now," she said. "I've got to get home and cook dinner. But tomorrow's a new day! You can do something fun then."

Later that evening, I sat down with my mother and sister. I was not taking any more chances. Tomorrow was our last day of vacation. We needed a POA.

"What's a POA?" asked my sister.

"Plan of action," I explained quickly. "This will include starting the day at a civilized hour—like nine o'clock." I gave her a pointed look.

After much back-and-forth discussion ("Oy, this is sounding like Chol Hamoed," was my father's comment), we finally settled on snow tubing. We'd pick up bagels and then head off at ten o'clock in the morning (yes, in life you have to compromise sometimes).

I drifted off to sleep that night with a smile, as I anticipated my fantastic and fun-filled day ahead. Ahh... vacation... There's nothing like it!

Midwinter vacation: Day Number Three

"I feel terrible," my mother said to me that morning. "But Grandma isn't feeling well, and I have to go visit her. I don't think snow tubing is going to work out today. I'm sorry, Sarala."

What?! Had I heard right? Would this turn into *another* ruined day of vacation? I couldn't believe it!

But I had enough decency to keep my thoughts to myself. After all, it wasn't my mother's fault that

Grandma wasn't feeling well, and I couldn't exactly blame Grandma, either.

Having nothing else to do that day, I decided to tag along with my mother and visit with Grandma, too. At least my mother took me to the bagel store on the way, and I finally got to have my long-awaited bagel breakfast.

And...a funny thing happened. What should have been *the* most boring and *shleppy* day...actually turned out to be pretty okay! Grandma was thrilled to see me, and I felt great about myself. We schmoozed and bantered together, my mother, grandmother, and I, and we really enjoyed each other's company. I also found myself relishing the relaxing pace of the day, which was so different from the frenetic rush of the other days when I'd been trying to pack as much as possible into my vacation.

I had—*could it be?*—fun on that day. Okay, so maybe *fun* would be pushing it, but I did have a wonderful time.

First day back in school:

It was great to see everyone and catch up with my friends after vacation. My classroom had even been repainted, which was kind of nice.

Yes, I know that school is supposed to be intense, and vacation is supposed to be fun. But I have to say that routine...ah... There's nothing like it!

Out-of-Town High

My stomach churned as I rang the doorbell. The worn-out leather nameplate on the door read "The Lichter Family." Although I had never met the Lichters before, they were about to become my substitute family for the year.

I live in a small out-of-town community in California. The town in which I live does not have a Bais Yaakov high school. From when I was little, I knew that I would have to leave town for high school; there simply was no other option. When I reached eighth grade, my parents researched various high schools in other cities and ultimately chose one that they felt would be suitable for me.

There was only one problem: the high school that

they chose was located in New York—on the other side of the country—and it did not have a dorm for out-of-town students. (For that matter, there were very few out-of-town students attending that high school.) So once I was accepted into the high school, we had another hurdle to deal with: finding accommodations for me. I had no relatives living in that area of New York, nor did my parents know anyone personally from there. After speaking to the school principal at length, my parents decided that I would dorm with one of the local families.

The thought of living with some perfect strangers, following *their* rules and schedules, and eating *their* food, was rather unnerving. After speaking to some other girls who had boarded with local families during their high school years, though, I began to feel at peace with the idea.

My parents were directed to the Lichter family. Mr. and Mrs. Lichter were supposed to be lovely people. All of their children were married, and they rented out their basement bedrooms to out-of-town Bais Yaakov students who, like me, were attending schools in New York. My parents and the Lichters worked out all of the technicalities, and months later, here I was, standing outside their front door.

Within moments of my ringing the bell, Mrs. Lichter swung open the front door and welcomed me into her simple, yet neat home.

"We are so happy to meet you," she said with a genuine smile. "Please make yourself at home here."

Worn out from the flight, airport scene, and taxi ride from the airport, I mumbled a half-coherent thank you and sat down on the couch. I glanced around the home. The Lichters did indeed seem like wonderful people, yet things looked so different in this house—so different from my own home. The house was much smaller, and the furniture seemed ancient compared to the modern look my mother had chosen for our own living room.

After serving me dinner, Mrs. Lichter led me downstairs to the small but immaculate bedroom where I was to live. After unpacking a bit, I spoke to my parents and then, utterly exhausted, hit the sack.

The next morning, I woke up in a state of confusion. *Where am I?* I wondered. *Oh, yeah,* I recalled. *I am in someone else's house, halfway across the country from my own home. I am about to attend my first day of high school.*

There was no time for a pity party, though, so I jumped right out of bed. I walked briskly to school, asking directions along the way. Walking gingerly up the stairs of the large school building made me yearn for the familiar surroundings of my small, warm elementary school.

The girls in my new class, I was to learn, had been together since playgroup. They all lived in close proximity to each other and were old friends. They weren't exactly snobby, but I did feel certain vibes from them. It was kind of like they were the "in-towners" and I was an "out-of-towner," so somehow we couldn't connect properly. Perhaps I was being overly sensitive, but I felt like the girls belonged to a tight-knit clique which I was not welcome to join. In retrospect, I realize that these feelings were probably unwarranted, and the girls really weren't a cliquey bunch, but that is how I felt at the time: the odd one out.

On that first day, I sat in my seat (I had found an empty desk at the back of the classroom) and watched as more and more of my classmates walked into the room and greeted each other like long-lost sisters. They were hugging and excitedly catching up with each other after the summer.

"How was camp? I missed you like crazy!"

"I know—I haven't seen you in forever!"

"Everyone, you must come and see pictures from my brother's wedding!"

That last comment elicited an enthusiastic response and sent a dozen girls clustering around one desk.

I felt like a spectator as I sat and viewed the friendly chatting and animated discussions going on around me. All the while I thought to myself, *Where am I supposed to fit into this picture? It looks like they are just fine without me!*

After a long day of school, I arrived "home," where I quickly retreated to my bedroom. I needed some quiet time to process my thoughts. What a culture shock I had experienced! I was a young teenager, and I'd never felt so confused, alone, and homesick before. I needed to talk to someone who would really understand. Yet the downside of living with a family—and not in a dorm setting—was the lack of "professional people," *madrichot* or mentors, who could help smooth the adjustment.

I spoke to my mother that night, but there wasn't much she could do to help the situation. She told me to hang in there and reassured me that things would get better. Underneath the brightness of her tone, though, I detected her tension. I was sure that she missed me as much as—and perhaps even more than—I missed her.

Living in someone else's family setting and adjusting to their routines and schedules was difficult. At the Lichters, I was expected to maintain quiet from 10:00 p.m., which wasn't so conducive to speaking on the phone after that time. I was also expected to do my own laundry and help out Mrs. Lichter a bit after dinner. Sitting with the Lichter family and learning the nuances of their household made me miss my own family terribly. Oh, how I longed for the familiarity of my own kitchen and bedroom!

But hardest of all was finding my place in school. In my old school, back in elementary, I had been a "somebody." In my new class, I felt completely lost. I tried to cover these feelings of loneliness and awkwardness with a façade of extreme self-confidence, which, girls told me later, made me appear aloof.

That first year was not easy, to put it mildly. Thankfully, my subsequent years were so much happier. I befriended a bunch of the in-town girls in my class, and I learned that the difference between "in-towners" and "out-of-towners" is not that great.

In eleventh grade, I spent a Shabbos with one of my cousins. I brought along some pictures from various school trips and productions.

"Wow," my cousin commented, flipping through the album. "You and your friends...you seem as different as night and day!"

"Oh, you don't even know half of it!" I laughed.

But was that true? I wondered. Yes, I was from out-of-town, and even after a few years of boarding in New York, I still dressed and spoke like an "out-of-towner." But once you looked past those externals, beneath the superficiality, were my friends and I really all that different from each other? We were all high school girls, with similar hopes, aspirations, and goals. We all craved acceptance, true friendship, happiness, and success.

I glanced down at a class photo and smiled. "Actually, we're really not that different."

Production Time

My popularity had skyrocketed overnight.

Months before, I had been assigned the senior job of "production head." But I hadn't realized just how incredible and all-encompassing the job would be, until production season rolled around.

"I feel like everyone is watching my every move these days," I said to my fellow production head, Blimy. We were sprawled on my bedroom floor with a package of colorful Sharpie markers and a stack of oak tags. We were attempting to create eye-catching posters to announce the production tryouts.

"I like the red-black combo," Blimy noted with an approving glance at the poster I was working on. "It's very sharp."

"Thanks," I said. "I mean, I feel like everyone is so into me these days." I smiled as I glanced down at my shoes. "I just got these shoes last week, and I've already noticed that about five other girls in school have shown up with identical ones! In the same color!"

Blimy closed the cap of a marker and looked up. "Sari, dear, I don't mean to burst your bubble, but your shoes are pretty standard-looking. If other girls in school are wearing them, it probably does not have anything to do with you."

I shrugged. It could be it didn't—but I sure was enjoying the extra fanfare I was getting wherever I seemed to be in school.

A few days later, Blimy and I, together with Mrs. Gross, the coordinator of the play, conducted drama tryouts in an empty classroom. With a clipboard on my lap (the night before, I had purchased matching clipboards for the three of us) and a pen poised daintily in my hand, I took notes and jotted down various ideas.

I actually felt bad for some of the girls who came into the room to audition. So many girls wanted parts in the play, and only a handful of them would be able to receive parts. Some girls looked as scared as lost children as they walked into the room and then recited their lines in voices that were practically shaky.

Like Toby Stern, for example.

Toby was a petite and shy tenth grader. When she hesitantly entered the room, I could barely hide my surprise. *I can't believe she's trying out for the play,* I thought to myself as I handed her a script.

"Please begin with the lines on the top of the page," I instructed her in a crisp voice. "Try to put as much emotion into the words as you can."

I hardly heard the words Toby said because I was lost in my own thoughts, mentally casting the parts for the play. When she finished reciting her lines, she handed me back the script and walked toward the door.

She hesitated there for a moment, fiddling with the doorknob. Then she turned back to us. "I just wanted to tell you something," she blurted out. "I *really, really* want to be in the play. I've never acted before, but I am willing to practice my lines and work very hard. It would mean a lot to me if I can get a part... Thank you," she added. She gave us a shy smile and then walked out of the room.

"Please make note of that," Mrs. Gross said to me as the next girl walked into the room.

"Okay, sure," I replied, scribbling it down on my clipboard. *But there is no way we could give her a part—for sure not a big part. She is so not the actress type.*

We had other girls who strolled into the room with feigned confidence and then recited their lines in melodramatic tones. But we weren't looking for those kinds of actresses either. We had a fantastic script, and I knew that the play had a lot of potential—as long as we made sure to cast the parts properly.

In my mind, I had already casted most of the parts. It was actually rather obvious to me which girl should get which part, and I was sure that Blimy and Mrs. Gross would agree. By the time drama tryouts were over, I had it all worked out. I smiled as I returned to my classroom and tucked my precious clipboard into my schoolbag.

"The play is going to be fantastic this year," I commented to the girls around me.

I was immediately inundated with questions. Everyone wanted to know what the play was about—and, even more important, who would be receiving the coveted main part. More than half the school was dreaming of being that actress!

"Come on, just tell us who's getting the main part!" my classmates probed.

"I would never spill the beans like that!" I replied, trying for a mysterious tone. "In any case, we haven't decided yet."

Of course, I knew exactly who *I* wanted for the main part. Simi Golding would be absolutely perfect for the role. She was an incredible actress, with a pleasant personality to boot. She had received big parts in previous school productions, so I was confident that she'd do an excellent job as our main actress.

After drafting the cast, Blimy, Mrs. Gross, and I had a meeting with the principal. That was when I discovered that the production heads did not actually have the final say—or even that much of a say—when it came to casting the parts.

We discussed the various parts, and our principal gave us a short list of girls whom she wanted in the play. I was okay with that, because the girls she listed were more or less good actresses anyway. And the one or two who weren't, well, I would do my best to ensure that they'd receive tiny parts.

"And for the main part"—she paused, and I held my breath—"I was thinking that we should give it to Toby Stern."

Toby Stern?! Had I just heard right? I leaned forward in my seat and glanced frantically at Blimy and Mrs.

Gross, who were silent. Well, if they weren't going to do the talking, I would have to!

"Um, I'm not sure how well that would work," I said, as tactfully as I could. I glanced down at my clipboard. "Toby is a very sweet girl. But I don't know if she really has it in her…"

That was my nice way of saying, "She'd be awful! The whole play will be a disaster if Toby Stern gets the main part!"

If I thought that my feeble response would change the principal's mind, I was absolutely wrong.

"I *do* think she has it in her," she replied. "I think she could—and will—do a great job."

I bit my lip. "B-b-but…" I stammered, as I slumped back in my seat.

"I want to ask you something," my principal said. "What is the goal of the production?"

To put together a smashing, incredible play. To wow the audience. And to have a great time while doing all this, I thought to myself. But I didn't think that was the answer my principal was looking for, so I remained silent.

My principal went on to explain the "real reasons" for production: to build girls' confidence, to promote *achdus* in the school, and to nurture hidden talents. It was hard for me to listen. *I can't believe that Toby Stern is going to have the main part,* was the thought that kept ringing through my mind.

I was in a horrid mood as I stalked out of the principal's office. Our play was doomed, and there was nothing I could do about it!

It was with very mixed feelings that I announced the parts for the play together with Blimy. Toby Stern was beside herself with excitement, of course. As we began rehearsals, I kept dreaming of Simi, who *should* have gotten the main part. In all honesty, Toby was an okay actress, and she obviously did put in a lot of effort to do as good a job as possible, but she just didn't have that polished dramatic flair I had been looking for, which Simi did. Coaching Toby in a kind and patient manner was a real *nisayon* for me, a constant test of my *middos*.

Before long, the thick red curtains opened before hundreds of women. I wish I could say that Toby came through and that "my" play was one of the best ever. But it really wasn't. It wasn't terrible, either. It was a mediocre production, with a mediocre cast. I was bubbling with frustration until the very end of the finale. *It could have been so much better,* I kept thinking.

Years of life experience have shed some light on this frustrating high school experience. Now, I finally realize that "my" play had indeed been an outstanding success. I can still recall the smile on Toby Stern's face as she posed for picture after picture together with her fellow actresses, and the confidence and the friendships that she—and many of the other girls—gained from "my" play.

I am finally able to see the truth of my principal's words. Long after the glamour and glitz of an incredibly orchestrated production will have faded from the audience's memory, the positive feelings generated from a project that fostered *achdus* and self-confidence in others will linger on.

A Once-in-a-Lifetime Experience

Y ou won't believe it!" my younger sister, Rochel, shrieked into the phone.

I smiled, because I knew why she was calling. It was an early evening in mid-February. The seminary replies for the seniors in high school were supposed to be arriving in the mail any day. Judging from my sister's animated tone, I guessed that she had received her reply and that it was quite a positive one. But for Rochel's satisfaction, I played dumb.

"What is it?" I asked. "Tell me the good news!"

Rochel could hardly contain herself. "I got into seminary! The one that was my first choice!"

"Wow! That's amazing!" I gushed. "I am so happy for you! You are going to have the most incredible year of your life!"

We chatted for another minute or two, and then Rochel hung up. She had more people to call and plans to make. I was left with my own thoughts.

I recalled the words I had just blurted out to my sister: *You are going to have the most incredible year of your life!* Would she indeed have the most incredible year of her life? Had my own seminary experience been like that?

My mind drifted back to my seminary days, a few years before. Sure, when I had returned home from seminary in Eretz Yisrael, I had *told* everyone that, "I had an incredible, amazing year!" In all honesty, I *did* have a pretty good seminary year. I learned a lot from some special teachers and enjoyed the meaningful classes and unique experiences.

Yet, looking back, I regret many of the choices I made during that year. I could have accomplished a lot more during seminary, had I only tried a bit harder. I could have taken the learning a little more seriously. I could have taken better advantage of the bountiful *kedushah* of Yerushalayim; I could have pushed myself to grow even more than I had...

To my surprise, I suddenly found myself blinking back tears. I loved my little sister so much—I didn't want her to experience the regret that I was now feeling. I wanted her to have not just a "pretty good" seminary year, but an excellent one that would be meaningful in every sense of the word.

On impulse, I grabbed a piece of paper and sat down at the kitchen table. The words just flowed out of me as I poured out my feelings to Rochel.

Dearest Little Sis,

Congratulations! You were accepted into the seminary that you have been dreaming of attending. I am so happy for you! You will certainly have a fabulous year—I am sure of it. But I don't want you to make the mistakes I made when I was in seminary, and then have to regret them afterwards, like I did. That is why I am writing this letter.

Have you ever heard of the expression, "She couldn't see the forest for the trees"? What it means is that if you focus too much on the individual parts of something—the "trees"—you might not realize that all the separate "trees" actually join together to make up something much greater—a large and magnificent "forest."

This happened to me when I was in seminary. Oftentimes I'd get so caught up when it came to the trivial aspects of seminary in Eretz Yisrael—my roommates, where I'd go for each Shabbos meal, the broken washing machine in the dorm, a leaky shower—that I ended up losing out on so much of the phenomenal elements the year had to offer.

The classes... It was only after my seminary year had been completed that I learned that one of my teachers was actually a world-renowned speaker! Now that I am facing "real life," it's no longer so easy to find the time to learn and grow. How I wish I could go back in time and sit through this teacher's classes again—this time, the right way.

How did I attend those classes back then, during

sem? I am ashamed to admit how often I dozed off during class. I was always so tired...even the most fascinating and inspirational *shiur* was often unable to compete against the waves of exhaustion that hit me on an almost daily basis.

This exhaustion, though, was my very own fault. I went to sleep crazy late each night, for fear that I'd miss out on whatever late-night action was going on in the dorm (usually nothing too exciting, but I could never be sure...). In retrospect, I wish I had slept more during sem. Contrary to what I feared, sleep would not have taken away time from my seminary experience; instead it would have added significantly to it.

Sleep. It's a magical element that can make the entire world (including the broken washing machine in the dorm) look a whole lot brighter. Sleep will also supply you with patience—for the lessons and for your fellow classmates.

As for Eretz Yisrael itself... Oh, how I yearn to *daven* once more at the Kosel and at Kever Rochel! I wish I could stand in these *mekomos hakedoshim* again and just bask in the *Shechinah* and talk to Hashem. Sure, I know I could *daven* anywhere and everywhere in the world. But there is something about *davening* in the *mekomos hakedoshim* of Eretz Yisrael...it is so much easier to have *kavanah* and to connect there.

And yet, how often did I go on my own to these places? Maybe a couple of times every few months. Should I admit to you how often I went shopping in Geulah? I guess I didn't want to give up my favorite pastime, and I just didn't stop to think about what I was actually giving up by wasting an afternoon on an outing to Rav Shefa mall over visiting the Kosel for a good Minchah...

So here is my advice: Look at the forest. Don't get hooked on the "trees"—the glitches and inevitable annoyances that will crop up. Your roommate may be very different than you, and therefore, it may be difficult for you to get along with her. The food may not be exactly to your liking. Your Shabbos plans may fall apart at the last second. The winter may be rainy and cold. But don't let these things taint your vision of the magnificent land and the boundless opportunities that are at your fingertips this whole year.

Instead, focus on the positive and take it all in. The splendid city of Yerushalayim, the stellar teachers, and the growth opportunities are all there for your taking this year. Take advantage of them all, as this is a once-in-a-lifetime experience!

May your seminary experience be filled with incredible growth, and may you have a wonderful year with no regrets.

Love,
Your Older Sis

SECTION 2

Between Friends

Left Out

The hallway was packed with seniors. Girls craned their necks, trying to see over their friends' shoulders so they could read the notice posted on the bulletin board. The sign that listed our senior year jobs was the focus of our attention.

We had all been waiting years for these jobs, and now that our time had finally come, we couldn't wait to see exactly which jobs we had been given. I was secretly hoping to be one of the *chessed* heads. That was considered one of the "best jobs," and it was given to the "best girls." I had worked very hard throughout my high school years to maintain excellent grades and to be friendly to all my classmates; I kind of expected the school to realize this and to reward me for my efforts with this coveted job...

I finally pushed my way forward and scanned the sign. My eyes drifted upward to the very first category: *chessed* heads. There were six names in that category... and none of them were mine. *It can't be,* I thought. *My name has got to be here!* I looked again, almost hoping that my name would magically appear, but it didn't.

So where *was* my name? Another glance told me that I'd been chosen to be one of the editors of the yearbook.

What a nerdy job, I thought. *I can't believe it! All my hard work over the years—and this is what I get? I am going to be the editor of the yearbook?*

I quickly realized that I had better escape before the tears came... I began walking quickly to the bathroom, but my friend Leah'le stopped me on my way.

"Hey, Ruchy," she said, "what's your job?"

"Yearbook editor," I mumbled as I walked on. I recalled seeing her name on the *"chessed* head" list, as well as my other close friends' names. *No wonder she looks so smug with herself.*

I finally reached the bathroom, where I allowed myself to dissolve into tears.

Why hadn't I gotten one of the "good jobs"? I wept. Why did all my friends receive the job of *chessed* head, but not me?

I cried for a few more minutes, and then pulled myself together, wiped my eyes, and prepared to face the world despite my disappointment. As soon as I walked out of the bathroom, I saw my friends huddled together with a few other classmates. All of them were talking excitedly.

Oh, those are the chessed *heads,* I realized glumly. *And I am not part of them.*

They hardly noticed as I walked by, so caught up were they in their own little world.

Later that night, I called my friend Faigy, but she did not pick up her phone. She finally called me back a few hours later.

"Ruchy," she said breathlessly, "don't ask! We are so crazy busy; you wouldn't believe how much work we have to do!"

"Oh, I am so sorry to hear that," I answered.

Faigy was so absorbed in her own world that she didn't notice the sarcasm in my voice.

"It's okay, we're managing," she said. "But I really don't have time to schmooze now. So have a good night...I'll see you around, 'kay?"

There was a click.

Have a good night...I'll see you around, 'kay? This, from one of my best friends! I couldn't believe it. *I'll see you around*—that was all?!

As the school year progressed, the situation only deteriorated further. Everywhere I went, I saw my friends huddled together, talking about their *chessed*-related projects—which, of course, I had nothing to do with. It was painful to watch my friends bonding without me—and even worse was seeing how others seemed to have taken my spot in the *chevrah*.

"I don't get it," I said to my friends one afternoon. "It seems like all of you are busy with your job twenty-four hours a day, seven days a week."

They laughed. "Yup, that's what being a *chessed* head all is about!"

I cringed. What did they mean? That being a *chessed* head meant leaving your friend out of things 24/7? That sure didn't sound like a great *chessed* to me.

I will never forget the Chanukah vacation of my senior year. I woke up one morning and tried making plans for the day. I called one friend, but there was no answer. I tried another friend, with no success. Finally, I reached my friend Chana.

"So, what's the plan for today?" I asked her.

"Oh, I'm not really sure yet..." Chana answered vaguely. "Um...my mother needs my help. Can I call you back a little later?"

"Yeah, I guess so."

She never called me back. But I did finally see her, when I walked into a local bagel store. She was sitting at a table with the rest of the *chessed* heads. Since they did not see me, I quickly turned around and left the store.

So that's where all my friends were on this lovely afternoon. The realization that they'd gone and gotten together for the day, behind my back, was very hurtful; I had never felt so alone and left out in my entire life.

Chana finally returned my call later that afternoon. "So, how was your day?" she asked cheerfully.

"Okay," I said curtly.

"What did you do today?" she asked.

"Nothing much. All of my friends were too busy for me." The words just slipped out; I couldn't control myself.

There was silence. I contemplated whether or not to tell her just how hurt I was. In a way, I wanted her to know how horrible I felt. On the other hand, I didn't want to come across sounding like a baby. What would I tell Chana? That I felt so left out? That all my friends were excluding me? That I used to love school but now I hated it because I felt like I didn't really belong to a group of friends anymore?

Finally, Chana spoke up. Thankfully, she seemed to sense exactly how I was feeling, without me even saying a word.

"Ruchy," she said, "you are a hundred percent right; we were wrong. In our quest to be the best *chessed* heads and plan the most *chessed* activities ever, we ended up excluding and hurting you."

I said nothing.

Chana continued, "We should have been more careful."

"Yes," I said, the pain in my heart forcing me to finally speak up. "It is not really like you. I mean, you're all my close friends. We've always been there for each other, we do everything together...do you know how painful it is for me to watch all of you get swept up into your own world, when that world doesn't include me? I don't think you even realized what was happening, but I have been very hurt."

Chana is a mature girl. She could have stammered a hundred excuses. She could have tried defending herself and saying, "We were crazy busy!" or, "This was our job!" or even, "But we had to do this! We were given this job and we couldn't have backed out!"

But she didn't. Instead, she said, "Ruchy, I'm very sorry."

And I could tell that she really was.

"I want the rest of the year to be different," she said. "I miss you."

"And I've missed you, and the others, like crazy," I

said. "I used to love school, but without all of you, it was just no fun..."

I can't say that things turned around overnight. The *chessed* heads were still busy with their jobs. They still missed class time together, had meetings, and occasionally arranged special activities that only included them. I absolutely hated the feeling of being left out of things, so each time this happened, I felt a pang.

But things did change for the better. Somehow, my friends came out of their own little world, and I began to feel a part of the *chevrah* again.

For midwinter vacation, we all went snow-tubing together. As we drove up to the mountains, we had a grand time laughing, schmoozing, and reminiscing.

It finally felt right. *Chessed* head or not, I did not have to feel left out.

It was about eight months later and again I found myself laughing and talking with my friends; only this time I was in seminary.

Chana, four other girls, and I were making plans to go away for an exciting Shabbos in Tzfas.

"This is going to be so much fun!" I exclaimed, looking over the itinerary we'd planned. "It'll be a real adventure." My friends all agreed.

I returned to my room to begin packing. Just as I was placing my Shabbos shoes into my Kipling duffel bag, my roommate, Esther, walked in. Esther was a kind and gentle girl, but she was very shy. And she wasn't exactly "Miss Popularity."

"So, Esther," I said cheerfully, reaching for my blow-dryer and tossing it into the bag, "where are you going for Shabbos this week?"

She sat down on her bed and began examining her fingernails. "Um...I'm not really sure yet," she stammered.

She wasn't sure yet? But it was already Wednesday night!

"Actually," she continued, "I...I was thinking of going to my cousin in Petach Tikvah for Shabbos. Do you want to come with me?"

I was quiet as I contemplated how to answer her question.

"Their apartment is a little small, but I'm sure they can make room for me and a friend. And it's really no fun to go alone..."

It's really no fun to go alone. Her words really touched me. She was right. It *was* no fun to go places alone...to be left out. There is no worse feeling in the world than the feeling of loneliness.

I thought back to the first few months of twelfth grade. I remembered how my good friends had gotten swept into their *chessed* activities, to the exclusion of all else...including me. And I remembered how miserable I had felt as I watched from the sidelines.

I couldn't do that to Esther.

I made a decision on the spot. "You know, Esther," I said, "a few of my friends and I are going to Tzfas for Shabbos, and we have room for one more girl. I would love it if you can join. And I'd be happy to come with you to your cousin for a different Shabbos."

Esther's face lit up. "Really?" she said. "I always wanted to see Tzfas! I would love to come with you!"

We all had a beautiful Shabbos together. I was a bit worried that Esther might feel like a tagalong, because she wasn't really part of my *chevrah* of friends, so I made a point to include her in our conversations as much as possible. And, to my satisfaction, I could tell that she was enjoying herself immensely.

It really is no fun to be left out. I'd learned that the hard way, and now I'd do my best to ensure that others would not go through that kind of experience.

Fad Diet

Pizzazz.

That is the word I would use to describe Esty. She is full of pizzazz, charisma, and spunk. She is glamorous and full of flair. Whatever Esty does in life seems so glorious and wonderful. Why, she can make a dentist appointment sound dazzling and fun—yes, you heard right—a dentist appointment!

Esty is the unofficial leader of my class. There is just something about her that somehow draws the rest of us in with whatever she's doing, silly or not.

One day, Esty arrived at school carrying a hot pink notebook, which she proceeded to place neatly on her desk. She flicked open the notebook and began reading something from it to herself.

I wondered what the notebook was all about. "Chumash notes?" I questioned, trying to sound nonchalant, despite the fact that I was sure it was anything *but* Chumash notes.

"Nope," she replied, hardly glancing up from the page. "This is personal stuff."

Personal stuff? If I was interested before about this notebook, by now I was positively burning with curiosity! What kind of "personal stuff" was written in her notebook? But I didn't want to sound desperate or snoopy, so I decided to play it cool and turned my attention elsewhere.

Thankfully, over the course of the day, the truth about the contents of the mysterious, hot pink notebook emerged.

"I am going to be up-front about this with all of you," Esty said to a group of us at recess. "I think you will figure it out anyway. I am going on a strict diet."

For emphasis, she pulled a Tupperware container out of her schoolbag. Inside of it was a bunch of perfect, round blueberries. Next, she pulled out a bottle of Poland Spring water. Suddenly, my bag of Dipsy Doodles seemed so dull...and fattening.

"What diet are you on?" Raizy asked.

"It's not really a specific diet," Esty replied. "I am actually seeing a nutritionist. Her name is Barbara, and she's fantastic. My mother has a lot of friends who use her, and they have all seen such incredible results that my mother suggested I give her a try."

Sheesh, I thought to myself. *What does she need to see a nutritionist for?* Wasn't that a little over the top? It wasn't like Esty was so overweight or anything. Okay, so maybe she was a bit heavy (and I had hardly even noticed that before she walked in with her hot pink notebook) but—a nutritionist? I thought it was a little ridiculous.

Apparently, though, the other girls did not share my feelings. They all thought it was a fantastic idea.

"Wow!" exclaimed Chani. "Good for you! I really admire you!"

Esty smiled smugly to herself as she gracefully removed a blueberry from her Tupperware container and popped it into her mouth.

"So, how often do you go to the nutritionist?" asked Yocheved.

"What exactly do you do there? Does she weigh you?" Miri wanted to know.

The others bombarded her with questions, and she patiently answered them all. As soon as the bell rang, we all scurried off to our seats. I took a side glance at Esty, who was now elegantly writing something in her pink notebook (she said it was called her "food journal").

My goodness, I thought, *there she goes again! Leave it to Esty to make dieting seem like the world's most exciting activity.*

At first, I assumed the whole dieting thing would be a passing, day-long phase that would quickly wear off, but that was not the case. Esty really kept at it, and she actually lost some weight and looked great. But the crazy part of it was the way the dieting buzz caught on with everyone else in the class.

I guess I shouldn't have been so surprised. This was typical with Esty, after all. The girls were so enamored by whatever she did, that it didn't take much for everyone to kind of follow her lead...

And so, no longer was it "in style" to arrive at school with a fresh muffin, potato chips, or a bagel. That was so...last month. The latest "thing" was to eat healthy. Ziploc bags full of cookies and chocolate bars were replaced with containers of salad and cut-up veggies. Cans of Coke were replaced with sport-top Poland Spring bottles and diet Snapples—that was a biggie. Practically everyone showed up to school with a diet Snapple. And no longer was pizza ordered at lunch time; only salads and whole wheat wraps from a local café.

This may all sound wonderful. What can be better than a healthy-eating trend? And truthfully, it really *was* a good thing...for those who actually needed to lose weight. But not everyone in my class needed to count every calorie. Like me, for example. *Baruch Hashem,* I've been blessed with a great metabolism, and I can eat normally and still remain thin. So, there was no reason for me to give in to this latest fad, and I promised myself that I wouldn't—I absolutely would not.

But at a certain point, I began to feel dumb pulling out my lunches and snacks that were loaded with calories.

"Don't tell me you are eating *pasta,*" commented one of my classmates when I pulled the lid off of my favorite macaroni salad. "With mayonnaise?! You have no idea how fattening that salad is!"

I was annoyed; I'd never asked for her opinion. And quite frankly, I didn't care how many calories were in the salad. All I cared was that it tasted really good.

"Actually," Esty piped up, "I was *just* discussing this with my nutritionist."

Everyone around her turned with bated breath,

waiting to hang on to the pearls of wisdom from Esty's nutritionist. "She told me that often, salads can be *the worst.*"

We all gaped in horror. "Really?!"

Esty seemed glad to have piqued our curiosity. "Yup," she continued. "Often, like at *simchos* or parties, the salads can be loaded with sugar and mayonnaise—like that macaroni salad right there. Well, in any case that salad is bad, because it's *macaroni.* So I guess that makes it doubly bad."

While Esty had not actually been trying to be nasty, the others looked at me—and my macaroni salad—with a look of contempt, as though my food were dirty, or perhaps a bomb waiting to explode.

Suddenly, my favorite lunch no longer looked appetizing.

So that is how even *I* got swept into the diet fad. Really, it wasn't my fault; I just wanted to fit in and do what the rest of the class was doing.

The next morning, I woke up early and carefully sifted through the fridge. "Hmm...what should I take for lunch?" I mused aloud.

"Why don't you finish off the macaroni salad?" my sister suggested. "It's your favorite."

"Nah..." I picked up a cucumber and a tomato. "Macaroni salad is *soo* fattening."

My sister just stared at me with a look of confusion. "Since when do you even know what fattening means? And since when do you care? You are a skinny pickle, and fattening food is the last thing you need to worry about!"

Granted, she did have a point, but I had no patience

to explain the reasoning behind my sudden dieting habits, so I just ignored her.

My sister continued to watch me as I carefully cut up my salad and mashed my tuna. "Well, I guess you won't mind if I take the last of the chocolate chip cookies, then!" she finally said, smirking. "I mean, you wouldn't want to go near any of this fattening stuff, would you?"

Later that day, as I munched on some carrot sticks, I thought of my sister, who was no doubt currently enjoying my mother's heavenly, soft-bite chocolate chip cookies. And then, during lunch time, as I nibbled on my salad and tuna, I thought of my macaroni salad in the fridge at home.

I should have smuggled it into school, I decided. *I could have always gone somewhere and eaten it while no one was looking...like maybe in a bathroom stall or something.*

On second thought, I had to scratch that idea—lunch in the bathroom; no, that wouldn't work. So for now, I would just have to stick to healthy food.

Glancing around the lunch table, I noticed that almost all the girls—aside from a few who were eating whole wheat bread or wraps—were eating salads. The topic of conversation, wherever I turned, was...salads, too, of course. And diets. And exercise. It was so utterly ridiculous. No one even cared to talk about the fact that the solos for the concert would be given out later that day. Or about the fact that we would be having a substitute next period. Because compared to the all-important topic of dieting, all else was simply trivial...

At one point, Esty glanced over at my lunch. "Now *that* looks like a healthy choice," she said approvingly.

"No pasta, no sugar, and no fattening dressings." She reached for her pink notebook. "What's in the salad? Can I have the recipe? It looks really good."

At first, I beamed with delight. But then I was struck with the ridiculousness of the situation. I am skinny. Very skinny. Why in the world was I watching my weight and dieting?! In style or not, I did not need to be on a diet!

I munched my way through the rest of my salad and then, just moments before the bell rang, I made a mad dash for the canteen and purchased a brownie bar. And when the others noticed me eating it (with a look of half-disdain and half-envy), I didn't even care.

Because, as I'd realized, I am my own person. I am allowed to have my own tastes and dislikes. And if my own tastes include something that may not be in the realm of the latest fad hitting my class...well, so be it.

The Ugly Monster

September 19

Dear Diary,

Okay, I'll admit it: I am jealous of Chevy Frankel. I wouldn't admit that to anyone else, but here, in the privacy of my bedroom, I can scrawl out the words. Of course, in public, I pretend that I am good friends with Chevy, and that things are all dandy and fine, but inside I'm going absolutely nuts!

I know. They say no one's life is perfect. But isn't there an exception to every rule? If so, then Chevy Frankel must be the exception to this rule. Chevy is gorgeous, a size two, and dresses beautifully. Of course, all of her clothing and shoes are brand-name and probably cost more than all of the wardrobes of the rest of the girls in our class put together. Her parents are wealthy and extremely nice people, too, and Chevy is smart, talented and popular...and has just about *everything* going for her!

Okay, enough ranting and raving about Chevy. I'd better go study for my Chumash test, which I bet Chevy will ace without even cracking open a *sefer*—oh, there I go again, talking about Chevy! See, she is even taking over my thoughts! Help!

October 7

Dear Diary,

I am so mad. I am seething! My principal announced the class representatives today. I was sort of hoping that I would be chosen—I mean, why not? I am a good girl, I do pretty well in most classes, and I (almost) never break school rules. I was actually looking forward to being a class representative. I figured it would be lots of fun, and hey, the recognition I would get wouldn't hurt, either...

But no, I was not chosen. And guess who *was* picked? CHEVY FRANKEL! The pure injustice! At this point, I don't really care so much that I *wasn't* chosen; mainly, I care that she *was*! Truth be told, I wouldn't care if any other girl in the entire class—besides for Chevy—was chosen...

Yikes... I can't believe the thoughts that are going through my head. This is so not like me. I am not a bad person. So what's going on? How can I be so jealous of someone else? I mean, jealousy is an *aveirah*—I have to be able to conquer it.

BUT CHEVY HAS EVERYTHING! IT IS SO HARD *NOT* TO BE JEALOUS OF HER!

October 15

Dear Diary,

Last time, I wrote about how bad I feel about my jealousy, but today I feel even worse. Here is what happened: Our math teacher, Miss Dick, is *really* strict—no one messes with her! Today's lesson was really tough and our class just wasn't getting it, so a couple of us started schmoozing. Miss Dick announced that the next one to talk would get a math assignment. Immediately, the class quieted down, but then, a few minutes later, the chatting began again.

Miss Dick dramatically opened her briefcase and handed an assignment to...Chevy Frankel! Could you believe it? Yes, she actually gave Chevy Frankel an assignment!

But you know...I wasn't even relieved that I *didn't* get the assignment. Instead, I was...I am almost embarrassed to write these words...I was happy that Chevy *did* get it. I thought to myself, *Serves that girl right. For once, something a little less than perfect is happening to her.* I actually found myself *smiling* as Chevy slipped the assignment into her Longchamp schoolbag!

And that disgusts me, and terrifies me to no end.

This is *not* me! It really isn't! I'm a good person—I really am! How did this terrible jealousy monster enter my life and take over like this? It's making me into a mean person; it's robbing me of my own happiness, and I can't stand it.

But how can I overcome this jealousy? Whom should I ask for help? Asking for help means admitting to someone how jealous I am, and that would be so embarrassing...

One thing is for sure, though: somehow, in some way, I must get rid of this ugly jealousy monster that has invaded me.

October 17
Dear Diary,

I don't want to be jealous of Chevy—*I really don't!* But why does she make it so difficult for me?! Each day at recess, a whole crowd of girls congregates at her desk to schmooze, while my desk is quiet. Wherever she is, there is action. And even the teachers love her; she gives them one of her classic, charismatic smiles and gets away with everything (well, besides for Miss Dick's assignment). It is so not fair!

Ooh, this jealousy is so horrible. I feel like an immature baby for being so jealous...like such a creep.

October 18
Dear Diary,

When I finished writing yesterday, I put my head down on my desk and began crying. I wasn't even sure exactly *why* I was crying. I felt miserable, because my feelings were spiraling out of control. I didn't want be jealous; I wanted to be a good person.

Just then, Ma walked into the room. When she saw me crying, she quietly brought me a box of tissues and sat down beside me. "What's wrong?" she asked.

At first, I didn't know what to tell her. I myself didn't know the reason for my tears. Was I crying because I wanted to be as pretty, smart, rich, talented, and popular as Chevy was? Or was I crying because of how jealous I was of Chevy, and of how horrible that was making me feel? But how could I have described to my mother that big, ugly jealousy monster that had taken up residence in my heart?

Instead, I just turned to Ma and asked her if she ever felt like there were certain people who just had *everything* going for them.

Ma answered that of course she felt that way! And many times she's felt quite jealous of such people!

I just stared at her in surprise. Adults struggle with feelings of jealousy, too?

Ma laughed. "Sure, adults struggle with jealousy! And as a person gets older, if she hasn't learned how to properly deal with those feelings, her jealousy just intensifies. In high school, girls can feel jealous of their friends' schoolbags, grades, clothing, talents, or jobs. But in adulthood, there's a lot more to be jealous about, if you haven't worked on overcoming this bad *middah*. People can become jealous about a friend's *shidduch*, their friends' homes, cars, children, and careers..."

I shuddered. I didn't want that to happen to me! I asked Ma how one can learn to overcome this terrible monster.

"First of all," Ma told me, "conquering jealousy is a continuous struggle; it won't happen overnight." Then she told me that the way she conquers the intrusive jealousy thoughts she sometimes has is by constantly reminding herself that Hashem gives each and every person exactly what he or she needs.

"If someone has something and I don't, then obviously that person needs it and I don't! And if I don't need it—then it wouldn't even be good for me to have it."

Ma also added that even when it seems like someone's life is perfect, you never know what is going on behind closed doors. Some people have their problems on their front porch, some have their problems on their back porch, and some people's problems are all the way in their basement! *No one* lives on easy street—not even Chevy Frankel.

Then Ma patted my arm, gave me a little squeeze, and got up and left the room. I stayed where I was. I had a lot to think about.

October 27

Dear Diary,

I'm working on it, I'm working on it. But trying to overcome jealousy is *not* easy. It is *hard* to control your feelings. Still, I keep trying.

And lucky for me, Chevy sure gives me plenty of practice opportunities—like today, when she strolled into school wearing brand-new shoes...again. I gave myself a whole speech about Hashem giving every person what we need—and I did feel somewhat better afterwards. But I won't deny it: it was still a challenge. A very big challenge.

I guess I have my work cut out for me. But that's what we are in this world for: to work on ourselves, right? And if the work is hard and progress is slow... well, at least I know that I'm on the right track. One day, with Hashem's help, I'll have conquered this monster. One day, I'll get there.

New Friends, Old Friends

Rivky

The persistent rain and dreary winds sent a chill through my bones. The scene outside reflected my mood. I was moving. Yes, I, Rivky Weingarten, was moving to a new town.

The whole thing was surreal. While it was exciting that my father had been offered an excellent position in our new town, I was nervous. I was about to attend a high school where I hardly knew a soul. In my old school, I was so established. Everyone knew me, I had a close-knit group of friends, and I was popular. The principal and teachers liked me. I was a somebody. But in this new school? I'd be a nobody, or more precisely, I'd be "the new girl." By high school, everyone already had their friends. I was surely doomed.

My friends and my older sister did not agree with my gloomy predictions, and they tried to comfort me.

"Before long, you'll be the most popular girl in the grade!" I was told.

Or, as my sister said: "You will not be the 'nerdy new girl'; you'll be the '*shticky* new girl' whom everyone runs after."

Easy for her to say; she was off to seminary, so my family's move hardly affected her!

In any case, I sure hoped they were right...

Aviva

Talk about random! A new girl in the middle of tenth grade?!

I was running late this morning and came dashing into the classroom just minutes before the bell. Huffing and puffing, I began telling a group of my friends about the crazy morning I'd had.

"Don't ask! First, I missed the bus this morning, and then I realized that if..."

It was at that precise moment that I noticed *her*. The new girl. She was sitting in her seat, organizing her loose-leaf, and listening intently to my tale. I did a double-take. Where had she come from? I just stared at her. I know it's not nice to stare at people, but I couldn't help it.

"So, what happened?" someone asked, urging me to continue my tale. But I hardly heard her. I was too busy staring the new girl up and down.

Her skirt was sharply pleated, and her hair was blown as if she was going to a wedding. A fancy schoolbag was perched neatly on the floor beside her chair. Suddenly, she looked up, and for one brief second, our eyes met. Then she quickly turned away.

Just then, Ettie Blumberg came over to the new girl. "Hi, I'm Ettie. What's your name?" she asked. Leave it to Ettie to be the first to introduce herself to this girl; Ettie is super friendly and always has a nice word for everyone.

"I'm Rivky Weingarten. I'm from Brooklyn," the girl said. "My family just moved here."

"Oh, nice," said Ettie. "It's always fun to have a new girl in the class!" She giggled lightly; the rest of us were silent.

"So, if you need anything," Ettie continued, "or if you have any questions about the schedules, just let me know."

"Thanks," Rivky replied.

At that moment, our teacher walked in, so I never finished my tale. In any case, I wouldn't have felt comfortable doing so in front of the new girl (who happened to sit right next to me). She just wouldn't get it.

The teacher began the lesson, and Rivky pulled out a crisp piece of paper and started writing notes. At one point, the teacher asked a question, and Rivky's hand shot up.

I was surprised. *She is already answering a question? On the first day?* It just didn't feel right.

Personally, I had no idea what the answer was, so I relaxed in my seat and listened as Rivky carefully answered the teacher's question. And she got it right!

My eyebrows narrowed. Really, I had nothing against this girl; but still...she was new, and if my observations were correct, it definitely seemed that she was on the snobby side.

Rivky

I just couldn't shake off the feeling that I was being watched—especially by the girl who sat next to me. Not just being watched, but being scrutinized and judged, as well. I tried to smile, I tried to converse with her—but no luck. Although I did my best to be nice to her, it didn't seem as though she was interested in being friends with me.

It's funny. All those who know me would never believe it, but I *could* be shy. Yes, I, Rivky Weingarten, could clam up from time to time. That is what happened during the first few days of school. I sat alone during lunch, and spent my recess break organizing and then reorganizing my loose-leaf.

It's hard being the one to take the first step in a new friendship. I wished someone would take an interest in me—not just to say a friendly "hi, how are you," but to really have a good conversation with me... It was a shame, because the girl who sat next to me, Aviva, really seemed like a cute girl...but I wouldn't push myself on her if she wasn't interested in me.

I generally was not one to wallow in self-pity, but at that point, I was feeling pretty sorry for myself. It seemed like I was in for a long year...

Aviva

Rivky got new, really cute shoes today. I wanted to ask her where she got them from, but I just couldn't find the right moment and way to ask, and so I never did.

It wasn't like I lacked friends. *Baruch Hashem*, I had a large circle of them. And my life was busy and full with other things, too: I had my grandparents' big anniversary bash coming up, for which I was in charge of creating a family scrapbook. Plus, I had one cousin who just got engaged and another cousin whose wedding was in another few weeks. On top of all this busyness and excitement, our teachers had been loading us up with homework and tests.

So why was I so preoccupied with thoughts about Rivky, the new girl?

I guess it was because I *did* like her, and deep down, I *did* want to be friends with her.

But how would I befriend her? And when would that happen?

Oh, it's never going to work, I decided. *And that's okay; I have lots of other friends. Who needs a new friend? Isn't there a saying about old friends being like silver?*

I had my old friends; I was fine. I didn't need Rivky.

Rivky

School was becoming a bit of a drag. The teachers were okay, but I missed my old friends like crazy! It wasn't that I was lonely—I did have a couple of "friendlies" in my new class. But I wouldn't exactly call those girls friends—not yet, at least. And not having friends in school took all the enjoyment out of my days.

The saving grace of my week was a get-together with my old friends. I met them in the city for supper and then a bit of shopping afterward.

I had a blast. We sat at a small table in the corner of our favorite café. We schmoozed and joked and laughed so hard, until we could hardly breathe.

My friends wanted to know how my new school was, and I didn't know what to say.

"I hope you won't make too many friends and then forget about *us*," one of my friends joked.

"No chance!" I replied.

Really, there wasn't. Like the plaque in my bedroom says, "The best antiques are old friends." That was totally true. There was nothing like old friends.

"I miss all of you so much," I commented as I boarded my bus—alone—to go back home.

"So do we!" they replied. But then they all boarded their bus together, giggling and joking around. They had each other. Did they really miss me? As they waved a quick goodbye from the window, I wondered.

I settled into my seat and pulled out my Chumash notes to study for a quiz we'd be having the next day. I halfheartedly flipped through a couple of pages, until I realized that I didn't even know which *perek* we would be tested on! I pulled out my phone. Who could I call to ask about it? Aviva seemed like the responsible type—and maybe, once I was on the phone with her, I'd ask her to study with me...?

Without stopping to think about whether or not she was interested in me, I found her number on the class list and punched it in.

"Hi, Aviva!" I said.

"Hi," she replied. Was her voice cold?

"Um," I began, "I just wanted to know...about the quiz..."

Do you want to study with me?

But the words got stuck in my throat. I coughed lightly.

"Sorry," I apologized. "I just wanted to know which *perek* the quiz is on."

She was quiet. Gosh, why was she acting so unfriendly?

"It's on *Perek Gimmel*," she finally replied.

And then the conversation was over.

Why didn't you just ask her to study with you? I berated myself. *Who knows? She might have been happy to, and you could have gotten off the bus, walked to her house, and had a great time studying with her!*

Instead, I had a lonely evening. Oh, well. At least I'd had fun with my *old* friends.

Who needed *new* friends, anyway?

Okay, okay, who was I kidding? I did need new friends.

Aviva

"Phone for you, Aviva! It's Rivky Weingarten!"

My heart skipped a beat; I felt like I was dreaming! Rivky? Was calling me?

As I ran to pick up the phone, my mind raced. Here was my chance! What would I say to her? *Maybe I should invite her to my house,* I thought. No, scratch that idea; I would sound too desperate. *Perhaps I should invite her to study with me?* Yeah, that's what I would do!

But then, it just didn't happen; my mouth clammed up and the words didn't come out. It's not like I didn't have the opportunity; Rivky asked me about the quiz, and I could have jumped right in with an invite. But I didn't.

What a wasted opportunity. What a shame. As I studied alone, I kept thinking of all the fun I *could* have had with Rivky. I could tell that she was a really cute girl—and lots of fun.

So when the teacher mentioned something about *another* quiz (what else was new?), I quickly turned to Rivky, not wanting to let another opportunity slip through my fingers.

"Yes?" she asked.

"Um...a pen, could I borrow a pen?" I stammered.

"Sure." She handed me her sleek Parker pen.

You did it again. Again, you blew your opportunity to become friends with Rivky, I mentally scolded myself.

But I have lots of other friends, I tried to argue back. *I could study with them instead. I don't need Rivky.*

Somehow, I couldn't buy that. There was no denying the fact that, despite all the old pals I had, I *did* want Rivky to be my friend, too. I had seen enough of her to realize that she was not a snob at all, and that she would make a wonderful friend. And, as Rivky was the new girl in school, I was pretty sure that she would be more than happy to be friends with me, too...

So what was I waiting for?

I decided to take the plunge. "Oh, and Rivky," I said, "do...do you want to study with me for the next quiz?" I felt my face grow hot as I waited for her response.

"Sure!" she answered with a broad smile.

I smiled back, and suddenly the day seemed brighter.

As the saying goes: "Old friends are like silver...but new friends are like gold."

To Forgive and Move On

There is nothing, and I mean nothing, like Shabbos in camp. The very thought of it brings a serene smile to my face, even during the long, frigid winter months. I've always been a real "camp girl." Sure, school is okay, but I wait for camp all year long. And my absolutely favorite part of camp is Shabbos.

I love the relaxed, stress-free Erev Shabbos preparations (followed, of course, by the last-minute frenzy when everyone suddenly realizes—at the same time— just how late it got). There's the communal exchange of blow-dryers, curling irons, and Shabbos sweaters in the bunkhouses... There's the smell of sweet shampoo, burnt hair, and fresh potato kugel filling the air... There's the singing of *"Lecha Dodi,"* the entire camp together, with our arms slung around each other, as the Shabbos Queen enters our midst... It's a beautiful way to begin what is almost always a beautiful Shabbos.

I say "almost always," because, with all of my pleasant camp memories of Erev Shabbos and Shabbos itself, there is one particular Friday night in camp that nearly ruined my entire camp experience.

It was the last Shabbos of camp that summer. Erev Shabbos passed uneventfully, and by the time Shabbos arrived, my friends and I were glowing, dressed in our Shabbos finest, with freshly blow-dried hair. The atmosphere was relaxing and sublime. A soft breeze blew in the air as the sun slowly set over the mountains and trees surrounding our campus. Since there were no cars on ground, we could really *feel* Shabbos, as campers, counselors, and other staff members mingled, wishing each other "good Shabbos" with a smile.

The singing during that Friday night *seudah* lasted longer than usual. I guess no one wanted the *seudah*—the last Friday night one of the summer—to end. When we finally did *bentch*, I felt a tinge of sadness; the summer was really coming to a close.

As such, I couldn't just go to sleep after the meal. I felt like I had to take full advantage of my last Shabbos in camp. A cluster of girls sat around in the dining room after the meal, singing, talking, and munching on peanut chews and popcorn, and I happily joined them.

The night wore on and slowly but surely, many of my fellow campers began retreating to their bunkhouses for bed. By 1:00 a.m., there were only a handful of girls left. We drifted out of the dining room and relocated to the floor of my friend Gitty's bunkhouse.

"Who's game for a walk?" asked Gitty suddenly, as if it was one o'clock in the afternoon instead of one in the morning.

The others were too tired. I myself had to stifle a yawn—but I didn't want to end the night just yet. "It is such a perfect night," I commented. "I'll come."

So it was just the two of us. We lazily walked around the camp grounds, finally settling on a bench outside Gitty's bunkhouse. I had always been so impressed with Gitty. In my mind, she was a real role model, a refined girl with beautiful *middos*. I'd always enjoyed talking to her, and now it was no different. We sat and schmoozed, and the time passed quickly.

By 2:00 a.m., I was just too tired to keep my eyes open.

"I must hit the sack," I said wearily. "Otherwise, there is no way I will be able to make it to Shacharis tomorrow morning!"

"Okay, sleep well!" Gitty said with a bright smile. "It was great schmoozing with you!"

I smiled back. "Good Shabbos; I'll see you tomorrow!"

Five minutes later, when I was in my own bunkhouse, quietly preparing for bed, I suddenly realized that I had left my jacket in Gitty's bunkhouse. I dashed outside, hoping to retrieve it before it landed in some lost-and-found bin; it was brand-new and I did not want to lose it or have it get ruined.

I tiptoed into Gitty's bunkhouse and poked around in search of my jacket. As I tried to locate it in the dimness, I could hear whispering voices coming from the back of the bunkhouse. I recognized one of the voices as Gitty's; she was obviously still awake. I was just about to call to her and ask if she knew where my jacket was, when I froze. I heard my name being mentioned. Could it be? Yes, it was my first and last name. She was definitely talking about me.

What happened next left a painful feeling of betrayal in my heart.

"She's really not that bright," Gitty was saying. "I heard that she struggles in school. I think she's in the remedial program or some kind of special learning track..."

I felt nauseated. Gitty was the girl I had always considered to be my role model. And I had just spent the entire evening with her! We had schmoozed and shared secrets, and I'd felt as close as ever to her. And now, just moments later, here she was, speaking terrible *lashon hara* about me.

Don't cry! Don't cry! I commanded myself as I turned to leave the bunkhouse. My jacket completely forgotten, I dashed to the bunkhouse door, trying to get to safety...

"Devorah?"

I whirled around. It was Gitty.

"Wh...what are you doing here? I thought you went to sleep." Her voice was shaking slightly.

"I came back for my jacket," I replied in a terse tone. "But I decided to forget it." And with that, I dashed back to my own bunkhouse and hid under the safety of my blanket.

How could she say such things about me? I wondered, as I tried to muffle my sobs with my pillow. It wasn't even true; I was *not* in a special program. Okay, so I had worked with a tutor a few times a week because I had

trouble with the textual learning; reading and understanding the *mefarshim* in the Chumash was difficult
for me. But that was it; my intelligence was fine! I felt
so betrayed by my so-called "friend."

I spent the next few hours tossing and turning, and
then finally fell into a fitful sleep.

At the Shabbos *seudah* the next day, I was spaced-out
and tired, with dark bags hanging under my eyes.

"Are you okay?" asked my counselor.

I wasn't, but I didn't want to tell her what had happened. So I tried to smile and said, "I'm fine—just a bit
tired."

During dessert, Gitty came over to me. She looked
nervous. "Devorah," she said. "We must talk."

But I turned away. *No! I don't want to talk to her! I*
thought. *That is the last thing in the world I want to do.*
There is no way I can ever trust her again!

When she came to my bunkhouse that afternoon, I
pretended to be asleep. It wasn't that difficult, because
I really *was* tired; moments later, I was actually fast
asleep.

The days passed, and I continued to avoid Gitty. It
was a shame, because this episode was really casting a
shadow on my final days of camp; it was hard for me to
enjoy *anything* anymore.

On the last night of camp, Gitty came to my bunkhouse and cornered me outside the showers. "Please,
Devorah," she begged. "Can you come out and talk to
me for a few minutes? Camp is almost over, you know,
and I need to apologize and explain myself to you..."

I just couldn't. I couldn't talk to her. I couldn't forgive her.

"Please?" she asked again, with a sincerity in her eyes that was impossible to miss.

"Give me a few minutes," I finally said. "And then I'll meet you outside."

My emotions were exploding. My pain was so raw; I was so hurt. Gitty's horrible words echoed in my mind again and again, as fresh tears slipped down my cheeks. *She's really not that bright...I think she's in the remedial program or some kind of special learning track...*

What nasty *lashon hara*! How could I just accept Gitty's apology and forgive her for what she'd said? On the other hand, Elul was just around the corner. *And it's not like I've never been guilty of speaking* lashon hara *before,* I realized. *What would happen if some of the girls whom I spoke about overheard the words that I said?* The thought was very discomfiting.

No, Gitty was not justified for what she had done, and it would be hard to forget her words. And yet...I did want to move on. How could I ask Hashem to overlook my own misdeeds if I couldn't forgive a friend for hers?

It wouldn't be easy, but it was something that I wanted to do. I walked outside and found Gitty waiting for me on a bench, fiddling with her bracelet.

"I'm so sorry," she said lamely. "I don't know how I said that about you, how I spoke that *lashon hara*. I never told this to anyone else. It just came up, late that night, and I was so tired...the words just came babbling out of my mouth. But of course what I said isn't true... everyone knows that..."

I looked down as Gitty continued to stammer excuses. But, as we both knew, there was no excuse for what she had done; she had been wrong.

"I just wanted to ask you for forgiveness," Gitty finally said. "I mean...Elul is coming. Soon it will be Rosh Hashanah and Yom Kippur, and...and...I need your *mechilah*."

"I know. And yes, I forgive you," I said with a strength that surprised even me.

When we finished that conversation, I felt like a heavy load had been lifted from my heart. I felt liberated; free from the hurt that had been holding me down; free to now get up and move on with my life.

Forgiveness is not always easy to extend—but the feeling of freedom it leaves in its wake can make it worth all the effort.

The Invisible Girl

Coming out of eighth grade, I had high hopes for my high school years. In elementary school, I was one of those girls who never really made it. I wasn't particularly talented, adorable, or smart, or popular. I just was. Esther Goldstein. Not exactly part of the scenery, but definitely not the type of girl that stuck out in any way.

So it was that I had such strong hopes and dreams throughout the summer, as I looked forward to entering high school. I would be given a fresh start, in a new environment. I would finally have a chance to be noticed; I would finally make friends. I would finally find my place and belong. With these hopeful thoughts and a carefully chosen schoolbag and shoes, I walked into ninth grade.

The very beginning of the year was a blur of navi-
gating around a new building, getting used to new routines, meeting new staff members, and learning the ins
and outs of high school. But as the confusion of a new
school and new teachers turned into routine, it slowly
dawned on me that all my hopes and dreams...well,
that's just what they were: hopes and dreams. Nothing
else.

Maybe I still have to give it some time, I thought.

But as the school year went on, I realized that time
was not helping. If anything, it was making the situation worse. Somehow, as everyone else settled into
school, I found myself once again on the sidelines.

Among the other girls, friendships began forming
and cliques came together. I so desperately wanted to
be accepted and part of things. And I did try. At recess,
I walked up to a group of girls and tried to join their
conversation—but they just ignored me and brushed
off what I had to say. Lunch time was no better, as I
struggled each day to find someone to sit next to.

I began dreading recess, lunchtime, and extracurricular activities. I never knew where to put myself
during these times. Where to turn? Whom to sit with?
Whom to talk to? Well, there was always the bathroom
to escape to, but that was not a long-term solution. *Why
couldn't I just fit in?*

In retrospect, I realize that I was an insecure and
timid girl who lacked self-confidence. And I did have a
particularly snobby and cliquey grade. Thus it was that
I found myself going through school feeling...well, un-
noticed. Invisible.

Torturous as recess and lunchtime were, class time

was not much better. Class would start with the teachers opening their roll books and drilling us on the previous lessons. I was not dumb, and I usually studied beforehand. But somehow, whenever I got called on, it was a disaster. The teacher would ask me a question, and there would be a dead silence in the classroom. All eyes would turn to me as the teacher waited impatiently for the answer. I'd feel my face turn beet-red from embarrassment, and I'd usually just freeze up and mumble, "I don't know."

And the whole class would hear it. So now, in everyone's eyes, not only did Esther Goldstein not fit in, but she didn't know the answers to any of the questions the teachers asked, either.

Sometimes the teachers tried to "help me out" by giving me a hint. That only made me feel worse. I did not need a hint! I did not need the teacher to help me out! I just didn't want to be asked a question in front of the whole class and be put on the spot with thirty sets of eyes on me!

I could never understand the purpose of these oral drills. All they did was bring on so much embarrassment, at least to me. Isn't that what written tests were for? So that you didn't have to be put on the spot in front of everyone, and if you didn't know the answer to a question, the whole class did not have to witness your embarrassment?

Maybe the class noticed and cared, or maybe they were too involved with their own selves to notice, and really couldn't care less if Esther Goldstein never seemed to know the answers. But in my mind, all eyes were on me whenever the teacher asked me a question, and the whole class looked down on me and thought I was slow. And this only made it harder for me to try to get accepted into a group of friends.

I never had much to do with my teachers, other than during those dreaded drills at the start of class. On the few occasions when I did raise my hand to ask a question, I always sensed a condescending kind of air coming from the teachers. Maybe it was only my imagination, but whatever it was, it made me feel very uncomfortable, and so I just stopped raising my hand.

And that's more or less how I went through ninth grade. I just sort of slipped through the cracks. I wasn't particularly talented, or smart, or difficult, so no one took much interest in me. Yes, the school did help the girl whose mother was sick. And the girl who came to school with a short skirt, nail polish, and lip gloss definitely did get lots of attention from the *hanhalah*. But Esther Goldstein? The quiet and timid girl who so desperately wanted and tried to be noticed and recognized, for the right reasons? Well, she just...faded into the background.

A few times, I decided to reach out to my teachers and let them know how miserable I was. But I always rejected the idea before I acted on it. How would I have approached my teachers? And for what reason should I have done it? Should I have told them that I was miserable because I had no friends and that I felt like a desk in the classroom? Should I have asked a teacher to notice me? No, I was not a *nebbach* case. And I was not about to turn myself into the object of others' pity.

And then there was concert time. I found the situation to be so ironic. While so many girls looked forward to concert, I absolutely dreaded it. Choir practice is fun if you have whom to talk to and laugh with during those long after-school hours of singing the same song again and again. But I didn't. And so those endless after-school hours of practice became pure anguish for me.

When the time came for the choir heads to give out solos, I tried out for one, hoping against hope... I actually had a very good voice, and I knew I could have done a great job with a solo. But of course I didn't get one. I wasn't gorgeous, popular, or brilliant. I didn't have a great personality, and I was not class representative or in charge of the grade *melaveh malkah*. And no, I did not have the confidence, or the charisma, to befriend the twelfth grade choir heads. Far from it.

So there I was, left to wonder: *why is it that the girls who shine have to shine some more?*

That day, the day they gave out solos, I came home from school crying to my mother. (I should insert here that Hashem blessed me with the most supportive family. I couldn't have made it through those awful years of high school without my wonderful parents and siblings.) When she heard what had happened, I don't know who was more heartbroken and hurt—my mother or myself!

"You're right!" she said. "It's so unfair! I'm going to call the school and ask them to give you a solo!"

"No, no!" I protested. "Please, Mommy, don't call! It will only make it worse!" I didn't want to get a solo because my mother had called up and complained for me! I wanted to get one because someone noticed me— and appreciated me and my voice.

This, of course, didn't happen. So, on the night of the concert, there I stood, at the back of the choir, where no one (besides for my mother) really noticed me. As the curtain closed at the choir's last performance, I breathed a deep sigh of relief.

In tenth grade, as the fragile and delicate friendships formed in ninth grade solidified, so did my friendless situation. I will never forget the day that the G.O. ran a "candy gram" program. For twenty-five cents you were able to send a "candy gram" to another girl and let her know that you were thinking of her.

While my classmates' desks became piled high with the "candy grams" they had received, I noticed that I had not gotten any. But then it got worse. I did get one—from a sweet girl in my class who loved to do *chessed*. As I read the note she had attached to a lollipop for me, tears formed in my eyes. So now I was the object of her pity.

But why?!

How are all the other girls able to make it, while I can't?! I thought bitterly to myself. I tossed the lollipop onto my desk, feeling as if I had just become stamped as an official *"nebbach* case."

As time passed, I found myself tagging along with Penina and Malka, two other social misfits, who were in a situation similar to mine. The difference between us was that they took out their anger and frustration by breaking school rules and codes of dress, while I was basically a good girl who would have normally shied away from such a group. But these girls were the first ones to make me feel accepted. They, too, were insecure, just like me...and so we stuck to each other.

As the years continued, Penina really slid down a slippery slope as she desperately tried to get some attention. Any attention. Even negative attention. Looking back, I am amazed—and oh, so grateful—that I managed to stay afloat and let go of those friendships before being pulled down too far.

Despite my misery, life moved along, and my high school years passed. By twelfth grade, I didn't even expect to get a good senior job. I mean, good jobs were for the girls who were smart, popular, and got solos in the past; not for girls like Esther Goldstein. As the year continued and girls made their decisions about seminary, I felt that familiar feeling of resentment inside me. The school did not inquire about my seminary choices, nor did they help push me in when I was rejected. It was only thanks to my parents, who managed to push me in to a seminary that was not exactly my first or even second choice that I had a place to go.

But here's where the *hashgachas Hashem* became so apparent. I boarded the plane for seminary, a crushed girl. But because the seminary was so small, I was finally noticed there. I finally made friends. I finally got to lead a school choir. And I finally fit in among the other girls.

My seminary year did not—could not—make up for the years of torture that I went through in high school. But at least it helped me realize, for the first time, that I was worth something, and that there were people out there who wanted to hear what I had to say. And it made me recognize that it was up to me to make the most out of my life. I had so much to offer to the world; I could not allow myself to simply wait for others to notice me, appreciate me, and bring me out of my shell. I had to do it myself, and that is just what I did.

After seminary, when I began working, I invested all my energy into my job, and it paid off: I became very successful at what I did. Finally, I was able to relish the feeling of true accomplishment and recognition.

Now, years later, whenever I bump into old classmates at weddings or other occasions, I can't help but feel the hurt and insecurity I felt in high school all over again. Seeing my old teachers, too, stirs up the familiar feelings of resentment inside me, as I remember how they did not reach out to me. But over the years, I have worked on myself to forgive my teachers and classmates.

I also feel a tremendous amount of gratitude to Hashem for the way I turned out. I look at Penina... Now that her life is in shambles, people are stepping in to help her. But why now, when it's almost too late? The whole situation could have been prevented in the first place. Why was no one there for her when the problem originally developed? Couldn't someone have stepped in to help years ago, in high school?

That is something I have learned from this whole situation: to never, ever take anyone for granted. I may have been the invisible girl in school, but for me, there will never be invisible people. I have learned the hard way how important it is to notice all those around me, even—especially—the quiet and timid people, and I try my best to ensure that no one who I know goes through the suffering of anonymity that I did.

And what of all the others, those "invisible people" that I don't know? That is why I share my story, in the hopes that my message will spread, and that maybe, maybe, I can open someone else's eyes to an unknown invisible girl out there...

The Class Snob

If there was any girl who fit the definition of the word "snob," it was Rivky Rose. There was just something about her that gave off an air of superiority to all those around her, which included almost the entire class. Somehow, it seemed that none of us were good enough for Her Majesty, and so, more often than not, she declined to associate with the likes of us simple folk.

Take the day I'd woken up late and rushed to school like a madwoman so as to be on time. I flew in just seconds before the bell, and let me tell you, I didn't exactly look my best. My hair wasn't yet made (I had stuffed it into a messy bun), my shirt was half tucked in, half hanging out, and, just my luck, the tights I had grabbed out of my drawer that morning had a big run in them.

So there I was, hustling to my seat, when whom did I have the "good luck" of encountering? Rivky Rose! And, just in case I wasn't self-conscious enough, she chose that moment to look me up and down—yes, from my messy hair all the way to the run in my tights.

It doesn't matter what Rivky Rose thinks of me, I tried to convince myself as I slunk into my chair, my face red with embarrassment. *So she thinks I'm a slob who doesn't know how to put herself together. Who cares?*

But I did care about what she thought of me. I cared very much! Why did I care? I am not exactly sure, but I did.

Just then, our teacher walked into the room.

"Can I please be excused?" I asked timidly. I hardly waited for her reply before dashing out of class so I could fix myself up. On my way out, I stole a side glance at Rivky. Yup, she was still staring at me, and I went from feeling dumb to feeling ultra-dumb.

"What a snob!" I mumbled to myself as I walked through the empty halls. I reached the bathroom and studied myself in the mirror. Yikes! I really did look bad. *Rivky Rose must think I'm nuts!* I thought. Of course *she* always looked neat and tidy; why, I couldn't recall *ever* seeing a hair out of place on her head.

I combed my hair with my fingers, tucked myself in, and tried to make myself look presentable. A few minutes later, I slipped back into my classroom. The girls in my class already had their heads bent over their *Chumashim* and notes—but lo and behold, one head was up and facing me. Yes, it was Rivky, giving me those "eyes."

Again, I felt my face grow warm and red. Couldn't she just leave me alone? Why did she have to make me feel so stupid?

A few minutes later, the teacher asked a question. I knew the answer, and enthusiastically raised my hand, hoping to get called on. From her seat in the corner of the classroom, I saw Rivky surveying the scene. Her hand was not up. She was looking at the class with this condescending look that seemed to say: *This is all so immature...* Again, I felt self-conscious, and I slowly lowered my hand.

Things like this happened all the time with Rivky Rose. The girl was *sooo* aloof. She associated with herself *only*, because the rest of us just didn't quite make it into "her league." In short, she was a snob.

So why did I even care? Why couldn't I just let her do what she wanted and "snob us all out" without giving a hoot about it? Sounds simple enough. But it wasn't! Because she really drove me and my friends crazy. She would give us her "eyes" and look us up and down, and in general, make us feel like two cents.

You can imagine, then, that when my teacher paired the two of us together for a project, I wasn't exactly thrilled, to say the least. To be more precise, I was mad! Out of all the girls in my class, *I* had to get stuck with the class snob?!

"There is no way she is going to agree to be my partner," I whined to my friend as we walked home from school together that afternoon. "I am not *good enough* for her!"

"Hey, give her a chance," my friend replied.

"Easy for you to say," I said through gritted teeth.

The next day, Rivky approached me. She wanted to

make up a time to work on our project. And should we meet at my house or at her house?

Well, there was no way I was going to invite her to my house. What if the kitchen was messy? What if my younger sister tried to show off? And what if my father cracked one of his corny jokes? I wouldn't be able to handle the shame.

"Can we get together at your house?" I quickly asked Rivky.

"Sure," she replied.

The next day I arrived at Rivky's house. I am not sure what I was expecting it to look like—but certainly nothing like it did. What can I say? Rivky's house was just...a plain old house. Like mine. And guess what? Her kitchen wasn't even immaculate. And her younger brother acted up. And...her family was just an ordinary family. They were all regular people.

During the first half of the visit, I was very stiff, and on my best behavior, trying desperately not to do or say anything dumb. I wouldn't even accept her offer of a drink. But as the evening wore on, I began to relax. Thankfully, Rivky did not give me those "eyes," and, amazingly enough, I almost felt like I was her equal.

Did I enjoy the visit? No, not really. But was it as bad as I thought it would be? Definitely not.

The next week, she came to my house. When my younger sister tried to annoy us to get some attention, I didn't even care. After all, Rivky's brother had also acted up! Soon enough, I felt myself relax. At one point, we even laughed together about something.

She is just a regular girl, I realized. *She is not in her own special league, like my friends and I always thought she was.* So why did she act like such a snob? Oh, who knew? But the important thing was that here, in my house, she was acting pretty nice, and...I was almost enjoying her company.

The next day, one of our teachers was absent, so we had a free period. We all gathered around and had an animated discussion about seminary (Okay! I know we were a few years too early, but it was a *fun* topic!). And guess who didn't join the conversation? Rivky. She sat at her desk, quietly reading a book and munching on pretzels.

I felt the frustration build up inside me. Why couldn't Rivky join the conversation like the rest of us? Why did she refuse to be a part of us? Why did she always have to do her own thing?

The shock came later that day when Rivky approached me as we left school.

"I wanted to ask you something," she said sheepishly.

I was sure that it had to do with our project, but I was wrong. It had nothing to do with that.

"My family is going to the country for the weekend," she said. "And my parents said I could bring a friend. Would you like to come with us?"

I just stared at her, too taken aback for words. Was I hearing right? Was Rivky actually inviting *me* for the weekend? And more astonishing than anything else— had she just referred to me as a *friend*?!

Rivky seemed uncomfortable with my reaction. "Umm...I know it's last minute," she stammered. "So if you don't want to come, it's fine."

"No, I *do* want to come," I said. "Let me just ask my parents first."

My parents granted permission, and I accepted the invitation. My friends were shocked (and perhaps a bit jealous?) that I was going away for the weekend with Rivky.

I pondered what had happened. Why had Rivky chosen me? Didn't she have any other friends to choose?

And then it hit me. She didn't. I was her only "friend."

Somehow, we had all mistaken Rivky's lack of confidence as snobby-ness. She wasn't "above" us and she wasn't better than us; she simply did not know how to join and befriend us! How wrong we had been, mistaking a lonely and friendless girl for a snobby and aloof personality.

As Shabbos approached, there were a few butterflies in my stomach, but I ended up having an awesome time. Rivky really came out of her shell. I got to see her true self, and I liked what I saw.

On the way home, I thought about how deceiving appearances can be. Who would have ever guessed that the "class snob" was actually not a snob at all, but a great girl—and a terrific friend!

I was just glad I'd allowed myself to see what lay beneath Rivky's surface.

True Strength

"Good morning, Shiffy!" called my mother. "You need to get up already—the bus will be here in fifteen minutes! Please! I really don't want to drive you to school this morning."

School? No, I couldn't go to school today. I did not have the strength to face school—or rather, a certain girl who would be in school.

"Can I stay home?" I mumbled.

"Why? Are you not feeling well?" my mother asked.

I don't lie. So I couldn't say I was feeling sick. At least, I wasn't feeling *physically* sick.

"I just don't want to go today..." I said simply.

"I'm sorry, dear, but that is not a valid reason to stay home from school." My mother's voice was firm. "I want you to get up and make the bus."

Having no other choice, I dragged myself out of bed and braced myself for whatever would be coming my way that day.

I walked into school with a scowl on my face. It was the absolute last place I wanted to be that morning. See, going to school meant meeting up with my so-called best friend Tzippy. And being that we were currently in the midst of a major fight...well, you can understand why I wanted to avoid her at all costs.

I'm not even sure how this fight started. My fights with Tzippy are usually like that. I do something small that she doesn't like; she gets angry and gives me the cold shoulder; I reciprocate in the same way...and soon the petty little argument has snowballed into a huge fight.

This time, it was something I'd said that had offended her, or could it be that I'd hung up the phone on her? Maybe I'd done both—I couldn't remember. But suddenly, by the next day, Tzippy had begun acting very cold to me and giving me abrupt answers to whatever questions I asked her. That made me start avoiding her—and by now, things were really bad between the two of us.

The day crawled by, and it was even more dreary then I had expected.

"Hey, did you see Tzippy anywhere?" asked Atara, one of my classmates, toward the end of the day.

I tensed up. In all fairness, Atara had asked a perfectly legitimate question. After all, Tzippy and I were officially "best friends." I guess Atara hadn't noticed that we were no longer on speaking terms.

"Um...I'm not sure," I stammered. "Could be she's at her locker."

"No, she went home early today," Faigy piped up. "You didn't know that, Shiffy? Her sister just had a baby, and her mother picked her up to take her to visit the new baby in the hospital!"

How painful. A major thing was happening in Tzippy's life—and I knew nothing about it. The tears welled up in my eyes. For months, we had been whispering about this, dreaming of the day when Tzippy would become an aunt... And now the baby was born, and I was the last girl to know about it?

Of course, I had to keep up my façade; I didn't want to sound dumb. "Oh, right!" I said, forcing a laugh. "How could I have forgotten? She left school."

Atara gave me a suspicious look; I imagined that she had seen right through me. "Everything okay, Shiffy?" she asked.

"Yeah, yeah," I mumbled. I walked away quickly, before she could see that it was otherwise.

The next day, Tzippy arrived at school in all her glory, with some photographs of the new baby. Everyone gathered around, squealing with delight, admiring the "*adooorable* baby."

I watched the scene from the side. Suddenly, Tzippy glanced in my direction, and for a split second, our eyes met. I quickly turned away.

Thank goodness, the bell rang just then, and Miss Perl walked in, putting an end to the uncomfortable situation.

Usually, I enjoy Miss Perl's classes immensely; she is an excellent teacher. But today I was unable to concentrate. *This is crazy!* I thought. *How long will this fight last? I hate being in a fight with Tzippy! It makes school such a dreary and miserable place for me.*

I was so desperate that I pulled out a sheet of loose-leaf paper and began drafting a letter to Tzippy.

> Dear Tzip,
>
> I really don't even remember how this fight started. Was it something that I did? If so, I am terribly sorry. But one thing I do know for sure: I hate being in a fight with you. I need your friendship; I miss you so much...

Suddenly, I looked up to see Miss Perl standing over my desk.

"Shiffy, are you with us?" she asked quietly.

"Um...sorry." I pushed the letter aside and returned my attention to my *sefer*. But I still couldn't concentrate. Now I was having second thoughts about why I'd written that letter at all! Why was I always the one to give in? Tzippy would stay on her high horses until I begged her for forgiveness. This always happened, in every fight of ours, regardless of who had started the fight and who was wrong!

Frustrated, I crumpled up the letter and stuffed it into my schoolbag. Nope, this sure wouldn't be given to her! This time I'd wait around until Tzippy came begging *me* for forgiveness! I was sure it wouldn't be too long; Tzippy had to have missed me as much as I missed her...at least I hoped so! I was sure that she'd come around by the end of the day.

But she didn't. And to add insult to injury, at supper

that evening, my mother decided to ask me about Tzippy's new niece.

"Shiffy, I heard that Tzippy's sister had a baby! That's so nice—the first grandchild in the family! They must all be so excited."

"Yup, they are," I said, hardly looking up from my grilled chicken. No one even noticed how down I looked, and they continued talking about the baby.

"There is this really interesting-looking recipe that I found in a magazine, and I've been waiting to try it out. Maybe I should make it for the *kiddush*," said my sister.

"Do you know when the *kiddush* will take place?" my mother asked.

"I don't know, and I don't care!" The words just burst out.

There was a stunned silence at the table.

"Sorry," I mumbled. "Just...could we talk about something else? Why is everyone so into this, anyway?"

"Whew! What got into *you*?" asked my older brother. I just glared at him in response.

Thankfully, the subject was soon dropped, and the rest of supper passed peacefully enough.

But my mother did not forget about what happened.

"Shiffy, is everything okay?" she asked me later that evening.

"Yeah, I guess."

"I mean, between you and Tzippy..." Her voice trailed off. My mother was not oblivious to Tzippy and my occasional fights. Sometimes she laughed and called our friendship a "love-hate relationship." Other times, our quarrels frustrated her to no end, and she'd complain that at our age, we should be past the petty fights already.

"Um...just the usual," I replied. There was no point trying to hide this fight from my mother; she'd already figured it out.

"Shiffy, this is out of hand!" My mother was exasperated. "If I recall correctly, you just had a little 'episode'—when was it?—two months ago?"

I looked down, slightly embarrassed. What was I to say? She was right.

"Well, it's all Tzippy's fault!" I finally blurted out. It was sort of true. Okay, so I was to blame a bit, too, but she was the one who had started ignoring me.

My mother didn't buy my response. "It takes two to tangle," she replied.

"Yeah, but what really gets to me is the way *I* always have to be the one to give in and apologize first! If not for that, we'd be in a fight forever!"

"Okay, and what is so bad about always being the one to give in and apologize first?" my mother asked.

"I feel like such a loser!" I answered. "I'm always the one running back to her and apologizing...regardless of whose fault it was."

My mother looked me in the eye and smiled. "Wow! Good for you!"

"Good for me?" I repeated. "More like, pathetic for me!"

"Not at all!" My mother's voice was firm. "The fact that you can give in—and pursue peace—is an amazing thing. It does not show weakness on your part; on the contrary; it shows true strength. And this amazing ability to pursue peace and be *mevater*, even when you're not necessarily the one at fault, will get you very far in life. Trust me on that."

I thought about those words all night long. And when I pulled out the letter from the bottom of my schoolbag, rewrote it neatly on a fresh sheet of paper, and gave it to Tzippy later that day, I did not feel like a loser at all. Instead, I felt strong, like I was doing the right thing.

I actually felt like a winner.

SECTION 3

The Curveball

Would've–Could've–Should've Syndrome

Would've. Could've. Should've. These are the three words that threaten to destroy our *emunah* in Hashem. To consciously avoid thinking these words when things don't go your way is not an easy thing. Yet, doing so is well worth your while, as my vacation in Eretz Yisrael demonstrated...

It was supposed to be the vacation of the century, the vacation of a lifetime. My family would be spending one glorious week in Eretz Yisrael. We were supposed to tour the country, spend one day up North, one day down South, and attend a relative's wedding somewhere in the middle of the country. We would walk the ancient streets, drink in the holiness, and take in the famous sights.

I was so excited that I literally counted down the days until we would be traveling. I spent the entire week before the trip packing—not because I had so much to pack, but because I was so absolutely excited about the trip!

The entire way to the airport—and during the flight—I dreamed of all the fun I would have in Eretz Yisrael. I just couldn't wait to get there already! After a long and boring flight, our plane finally landed in Tel Aviv. I jumped up, grabbed my carry-on, and got ready to sprint off the plane. I was itching to start touring the marvelous country already.

"Patience, honey," the stewardess told me. "It's going to take some more time. Business and first class disembark the aircraft first."

Well, my family had traveled economy, so we had to wait.

When we *finally* got out of the airport, I was brimming with ideas. "Can we go to the Kosel?" I asked my mother. "And then can we walk around the Old City? Then we can go to Geulah, and when we finish that, maybe we can—"

"Slow down, Sarala!" my sister interrupted my dream itinerary. "The only thing I want right now is a bed!"

A *bed*?! She wanted to go to *sleep*?! When we had just arrived in Eretz Yisrael?!

But sure enough, that is precisely what happened. We went to the apartment we were staying at, ate some leftover deli sandwiches, and then headed to bed! What a disappointment. I growled the whole night and barked at my siblings. I was annoyed over the wasted opportunity. There was so much we *could've* been do-ing; we *should've* been doing so many exciting things...

To make matters even worse, it rained the next day, so we had another sluggish day. On the third day (almost halfway through our trip), my little brother had a stom-achache, so we were off to another late start. There was also a misunderstanding, and the driver who was sup-posed to be taking us around never showed up. I was once again filled with thoughts of *would've-could've-should've.*

We could have done so much more that day! What a wasted opportunity! My once-in-a-lifetime trip was turning into a fast-disappearing and disappointing week.

That night, after we had gotten back to our apart-ment, I was so aggravated that I burst into tears. The sheer irony! Here I was, on the dream vacation of a life-time, and I was crying.

And that's how my father found me—staring out the living room window, tears of frustration streaming from my eyes.

"What's wrong, Sarala?" he asked.

Sheepishly, I explained to him the reason for my tears. "We should have done so much more in Eretz Yisrael at this point in our trip. So much time was wasted for no reason, and we only have a few days left here... It's not fair!"

"But Sarala," my father pointed out gently to me, "if you continue with this line of thinking, then your *entire* trip will be ruined. Because instead of enjoying what-ever we *do* get to do and where we *do* go, you'll keep thinking of all that we *should have* done but didn't."

At first, I shrugged off his words and continued to

wallow in self-pity. *Why can't my family just get their act together?* I continued to fume. But the more I thought along those lines, the more I realized that I was actually making my own self upset. The rest of my family did not seem to share my upset feelings—they actually seemed very happy, living up each moment of our trip.

You, too, can enjoy the rest of the trip, a niggling voice inside of my head told me. *It's really up to you and your attitude. You can't relive the past few days or change whatever already happened. But you can take Tatty's advice to heart and allow yourself to enjoy whatever time you still have left on the trip. You just have to make a conscious decision to do it...*

It wasn't easy to snap out of my rut—to remind myself that Hashem runs the world and that every disappointment, whether little or big, comes from Him and is ultimately for the good. But when I set my mind to changing my attitude and put a smile on my face, the world looked a whole lot brighter—and the last few days of the trip turned out to be unbelievably enjoyable.

And when I returned home and my classmates bombarded me with the "How was your trip?" questions, I was able to smile and answer in all honesty, "It was amazing!"

(At least, most of it was!)

The Bright Side

A re we there?" I asked my seatmate groggily, having just woken up from a catnap on the bus.

"Almost," she answered. We were on the bus home from camp. Although it had been a wonderful summer, I couldn't wait to get home. I'd see my parents, dump my entire suitcase in the laundry room, take a long hot shower (without waiting on line), and then crawl into my own comfortable bed. Just the thought of my bed made me smile... Then, I would wake up to a delicious supper and tell my parents all about my terrific summer.

When we arrived at the bus stop, I anxiously looked around for my parents—but they weren't there. After a few minutes of waiting, I finally noticed my older sister.

"Hi, Atara!" my sister called to me.

I grinned and ran over to her. "Hi, Devorah! Where are Mommy and Daddy?"

She was quiet for a moment. "Mommy wasn't feeling up to coming this morning, and Daddy...couldn't come either," she finally said. "But aren't you happy to see me?"

Well, yes, I was happy to see Devorah, but I definitely would have preferred to see my parents. Feeling the faintest niggling of anxiety in my stomach, I got into the car and we drove home in silence. My sister seemed very out of it, not like her usual vibrant self, and the niggling in my gut intensified just a bit.

"I'm home!" I called out when I walked into the house. My mother came out of the kitchen and greeted me. "Where's Daddy?" I asked.

"Um...he's away on a business trip," my mother answered. "I'll tell you about it later." She looked very uncomfortable.

Later that evening, my mother sat me down to explain what was really happening: My parents were getting divorced. Daddy was indeed away, but not on a business trip. He had moved away and would never return to our home.

I was shocked.

My first thought was: *I've always pitied the girls who come from broken families, and now I'm suddenly going to be joining that crowd?!*

Then my mind began whirling with questions. What did this mean? How could a family run without a father? Where did Daddy live now? When would I see him?

My future had suddenly turned into a hazy blur. I

tossed and turned the entire night, now wishing I could turn back the clock and be lying on my thin mattress in camp rather than in my own bed at home; at least in camp I had not had the worry of the world on my shoulders like this.

I finally did fall into a fitful sleep. As soon as I woke up the next morning, the stark truth hit me like a truck: My family was breaking apart.

The next few days were excruciating for me as I worried about all the ramifications of my family's new status. I'd always considered myself to be as typical as they came. I had loads of friends and was part of the "in" crowd at school. Now, I would suddenly turn into the talk of town, and the girl that everyone pitied.

I had always been very excited for the first day of school. Greeting friends and seeing girls whom I hadn't seen all summer was always lots of fun. But this year, I dreaded going back to school, because of the awful baggage that had been placed upon me. *Will I suddenly turn into my grade's* nebbach *case?* I wondered. *Will my teachers feel extra bad for me?*

The first day of school was very hard. I was paranoid that people were talking about me and kept looking over my shoulder to make sure no one was pointing in my direction.

"Hey, Atara," my friend Rochel greeted me at recess. "How was your summer? How was camp?"

I hesitated. *What should I say?* I decided to carry on like all was normal. I answered my friend's questions and we began talking about camp. A few other friends joined our conversation. At one point I found myself repeating a funny story that had happened in camp.

The girls laughed along with me. Then, Ricky shared the story about the fire drill that happened in camp when she was in the shower, and Chani told us about her brother's wedding in London.

As our schmoozing continued, it dawned on me that even though my parents had gotten divorced, life still went on. Here I was, talking about completely regular things with my friends, and it didn't seem like anyone was treating me any differently than usual. They probably had heard about the divorce, but it seemed that they had gotten over the news already. That's how life goes, I realized; despite my earth-shattering news, there were already newer and more important things to talk about than Atara's parents' divorce.

After the reality of the divorce hit, I decided that I had two ways to go about my life. I could become depressed, make myself miserable, slack off in school, and become an outcast. But I realized that by doing so, I'd only be hurting myself. And that is why I decided to go with the second option: to go on with my life and become an even stronger person because of my situation.

In theory, that sounds like a wonderful idea—but in reality, it wasn't easy at all. There were times when I wanted to hide under my covers and completely cut myself off from the world because of how awful I felt about the whole situation. Shabbos was very difficult. Before the divorce, I had hated waiting for my father to return home from shul so we could start the meal; after the divorce, I longed for the hungry wait for Daddy. Before the divorce, we had always hosted many guests for Yom Tov; after the divorce, I found myself—for the first time in my life—a guest in someone else's home. Watching neighbors' and friends' fathers leading their meals—meals in which I and my mother and siblings were participants—was too painful for words.

There was another aspect of the divorce that was very difficult for me. I sometimes wondered if I had played a part in my parents' divorce at all. Was I at fault for it? Had I done things differently, could the divorce have been prevented?

One Friday evening, I finally verbalized my thoughts to my mother.

"Mommy, is it my fault?" I asked quietly.

"Atara, is *what* your fault? That you are about to spill that entire salad onto the floor? Yes, if you don't space in, it will be your fault!"

I smiled at her joke, but then became instantly serious.

"No, Mommy, the divorce," I said somberly.

My mother led me to the couch and sat down beside me. "Atara, sweetheart, I want you to know that the divorce has absolutely nothing to do with you."

We had a long and serious conversation, and afterwards I went to sleep feeling like a large brick had been removed from my heart. I learned from that conversation that sometimes it's best to talk things over.

Despite the obstacles and hardships I experienced, I forged ahead in my mission to make the most of my life, regardless of my situation. One of the best things

I did was to befriend some girls who were facing the same challenge as I was. Although all my friends were thankfully supportive and understanding of me and my situation, they didn't—couldn't—get it completely. They occasionally made awkward and insensitive comments, and though I knew that the comments weren't intentional, it wasn't always easy to shrug them off.

These other friends, though, whose parents were also divorced, understood me only too well. We were able to confide in each other and have serious conversations about things that other girls just wouldn't relate to.

Throughout everything, I tried to see the bright side. Okay, so maybe at times there wasn't much brightness to be seen, but I always tried to find that silver lining whenever possible. I made the most of each Shabbos with my father, and enjoyed meeting and befriending his new neighbors. In fact, many of my classmates lived near my father, and I enjoyed seeing them on the weekends that I spent together with him. Also, before the divorce, Daddy had always been so busy, but now I was actually able to spend more quality time with him and develop a better relationship with him.

I suppose I could have been angry at my parents, but I realized that anger would do me no good. Also, I realized that as hard as the divorce was for me, it was so much harder on my mother, and I tried to be there for her. Over the years, my mother and I became much closer. I learned to recognize and appreciate all that she did to make our family life as normal and as comfortable as possible.

My mother is very musical, and often plays music for us. She taught me how to play the guitar, and whenever I felt down, or like I was going to explode, I let out my frustration by playing the guitar. It always helped me calm down.

Sometimes I'd worry about the future. If my parents got divorced, perhaps the same would happen to me? The thought scared me to no end. Finally, one day, I approached a teacher to discuss it with her.

"Atara," she said, "I know you, and you are a truly wonderful person. The divorce has nothing to do with you as a person, and you should not worry about this. I am sure that a beautiful future awaits you, *b'ezras Hashem.* I think that whoever marries you is a very, very lucky person. Going through such a difficult situation has molded you into a stronger and kinder person. And it is precisely these traits that will help you build a wonderful marriage one day, with Hashem's help."

Her words did indeed reassure me and allowed me to look forward to a brighter future.

Now it is years later. People marvel at the person I've become. As for me...I am just so grateful. I'm grateful to Hashem, for the strength He gave me to carry on; to my parents, for keeping things as pleasant as possible, even under the circumstances; and to my teachers and the others in my life who helped me deal with my challenge.

Indeed, I'm grateful to have grown from this situation in a way that really made me into a kinder, more sensitive, and more mature person.

Postscript:

My mother is an incredible woman. I was in high school when I wrote her this letter:

Dear Mommy,

There are times I get frustrated, times when I get angry and yell. It may seem like I don't appreciate all that you are doing for me. But really, it's just a build-up of my own frustration that unfortunately can seem to be directed at you. From your patience, though, I know that you understand this and that you do know how much I love you.

The divorce was very hard on me. But I realize that however hard it was on me, it was that much harder for you. Despite this, you put yourself aside and focused on the family. You forged ahead with an enormous amount of courage and kept things as pleasant and as calm as possible—because you love us so much.

I don't know how you do it. Each morning, you wake up with a smile on your face and spend the next hour juggling a trillion things to get everyone out the door. Then you pull yourself together, grab a quick bite, and head off for a long and tiring day of work. When you come home, there is hardly a second to breathe. The circus continues: homework, cooking, laundry, shopping, talking to us and giving us your full attention, phone calls, and Shabbos plans (which are often a sore point). Since you are doing all this by yourself, you never have a chance to think about your own needs.

This continues day after day. And now I finally pause to reflect on all that you do. To the world, you may seem like a "regular" woman who's divorced and raising seven children. But I know the truth: You are far from regular. You are a superwoman, devoting your life to your children, day in, day out, always with a smile on your face.

So I want to thank you. But how? There aren't any words. And no gift in the world would suffice either.

The only thing I can do to thank you and show my appreciation, is to continue in your special ways. I can only hope that one day, I will grow up to be as great a person as you.

With lots of love,

Your daughter

A Sweet Life Notwithstanding

Slam. The screen door of my bunkhouse slammed shut behind me, and I took in the slightly musty smell with an appreciative smile. Summer in camp—it had finally arrived!

After dragging my luggage into my bunkroom, I plopped down on my bed for a well-deserved break. My unpacking could wait a few minutes.

The girl next to me was a few steps ahead. She had already unpacked her belongings and was lying on her neatly-made bed, reading a magazine.

"Hi!" she introduced herself. "My name is Leah."

"Nice to meet you," I replied. "I'm Esther Raizy."

"Hey, think I could borrow your MP3 player?" she asked. "What kind of music do you have on it?"

I quickly busied myself with unpacking my duffel bag, any thoughts about taking a break forgotten. *Leah had mistaken my insulin pump for an MP3 player!*

I wasn't sure how to respond to my new roommate. It wasn't like I planned on keeping my condition a secret. But I just didn't feel it was the most opportune time to explain that my "MP3 player" really was an insulin pump...

I glanced at Leah, who was still looking at me expectantly. "Um...no, I need it...sorry," I told her.

Leah returned to her magazine and the conversation ended, albeit with some coolness in the air.

Later that afternoon, Leah ran over to me in the dining room, her face red. "I can't believe what I said to you!" she apologized. "I just found out... I feel terrible... I asked if I could use your..."—she hesitated for a moment—"thing. I didn't realize what it really was. I thought—"

I cut her off. "Leah, it's fine. How were you supposed to know that I had diabetes? Don't worry about it!"

Leah seemed shocked by the way I had mentioned my condition so casually. But I just gave her a pleasant smile. My diabetes had never been—and never will be—a secret. It is just part of who I am...

I was only six years old when I was diagnosed with diabetes.

I barely remember my pre-diabetes existence. I recall, shortly before I was diagnosed, being thirsty, drinking a lot of water, and going to the bathroom very often. When I began to lose weight quite suddenly, my parents took me to my pediatrician, who immediately conducted a battery of tests. When one test revealed that my blood sugar was extremely high, I was admitted to the hospital. I didn't know what blood sugar was at the time, but I did know that I wasn't feeling well at all. A short while later, I was diagnosed with diabetes.

Since then, I have never been secretive about my condition. My diabetes was simply one small part of me. It wasn't like I was "Esther Raizy with diabetes." I was "Esther Raizy...oh, and by the way, I have diabetes." Because I was so open and easygoing about my condition, my friends didn't really think twice about it. The way I viewed it, just as some girls wore glasses and some wore braces, *I* wore an insulin pump. The fact that I had diabetes never affected my social standing; I was a popular student, did well academically, and was even chosen as the G.O. president.

Admittedly, having diabetes as a teen did present its challenges. My everyday food choices took more time and consideration than the average teen's did; I had to make careful calculations about the sugar content in everything I ate. If I didn't know what was inside a certain food item, I either had to ask around until I found out, or stay away from that food. At times, when I was not accurate in my assessment and I ingested too much sugar, I would get a "high" and feel dizzy, anxious, and irritable.

Other times, when my blood sugar was too low, usually because I hadn't eaten enough sugar, I would get what's called a "low" and begin experiencing extreme drowsiness, as well as hunger or nausea.

But I quickly learned how to respond to my body's reactions by adjusting my food intake and insulin accordingly; I can honestly say that my diabetes didn't really play a major role in my life.

When I arrived in seminary, I was once again faced with a group of new girls who didn't know me. I knew I couldn't take care of myself properly if my diabetes was hidden from the world; I needed my roommates to be on the alert in case I had a diabetic emergency, *chas v'shalom*. And it wasn't like I was ashamed of my condition, so there really was no reason for me to hide it from anyone. On the other hand, though, I felt silly making a grand announcement about my diabetes to my brand-new roommates.

Instead, I turned to my close friend. "Can you do a favor for me and tell the other girls about my diabetes?" I asked her. "Don't make a big deal about it; just mention it in passing. I want them to know."

Baruch Hashem, the girls took the information in stride, and I had a wonderful year in seminary, with hardly any awkward situations cropping up because of my condition.

After seminary, I entered the *parshah* of *shidduchim* with no small amount of reservations. But Hashem helped me find my *bashert* easily, and we got married shortly after I returned home from seminary. Thankfully, my husband was not at all bothered by the fact that I have diabetes. Today, I am happily married, with two healthy children, and I work at two different jobs.

My message to those who may know someone with diabetes is this: Treat that person like you would treat anyone else. Realize that this person is exactly like you. She has likes and dislikes just as you do; she is capable just as you are; she will *b'ezras Hashem* get married and have children just like you will.

And to the teens with diabetes: As long as you keep your diabetes under control, realize that there is *nothing*—and I mean nothing—you can't do in life.

Charity Begins at Home

From the moment I walked into the Hirsch home, I knew that something was amiss. Coats, shoes, and toys were scattered in the usually gleaming front hallway. The two oldest children had very serious expressions on their faces, and the youngest Hirsch child looked like she had been crying. I had babysat at the Hirsches for almost three years now, and I had *never* seen them—or the house— like this before.

"I'll be down in a minute!" called Mrs. Hirsch from upstairs.

I chatted with the children until she finally came down a few minutes later, looking tense and exhausted.

"I don't really want this to become public knowledge," she began, "but my husband is currently experiencing some health problems. He's been in and out of the hospital for the past couple of weeks... Life in our home has been a little crazy."

I was shocked. I had no idea that anything had been amiss in their family! Mr. Hirsch was such a vibrant man; it was hard to believe that he was sick.

"I am actually running to the hospital right now," Mrs. Hirsch continued as she retrieved her large designer pocketbook from the hall closet. "Until now, my sisters-in-law had been pitching in with the babysitting, but no one was available tonight..."

"It's no problem," I stammered. "I am happy to help out. Is there anything else I can do for you?"

Uncharacteristically, Mrs. Hirsch asked me to fold some laundry, wash the dishes, and tidy her house. And then she was gone.

I took a deep breath. This would be no simple babysitting job, no siree. The children were sad and uncooperative. Ultimately, I decided to go with the flow and let *them* lead the show. They wanted pizza bagels for supper? No problem. I also let them stay up past their bedtime.

Before going to bed, Shani, the oldest Hirsch child, whispered, "I miss my Tatty."

"It must be so hard," I replied. That had been her first mention of her father all evening. In general, Shani was just like her mother: private and reserved. She was the kind of kid who kept everything to herself.

I spoke to her for a few minutes after tucking her into bed. I did not probe her for information (although, to be honest, I *was* burning with curiosity about the details of the situation), instead letting her do whatever talking she wanted to do. I understood that my role was to listen to her, empathize, and serve as moral support. And though I wasn't quite sure what the right responses were to whatever she did tell me, I told myself that one usually can't go wrong with sincere, tactful words that come straight from the heart.

Hours later, Mrs. Hirsch returned from the hospital, appearing even more worn-out than before. "I'm sorry I'm late," she apologized, as she collapsed into an armchair. "But I just couldn't leave any earlier."

"No trouble at all," I assured her. "Please, call me any time."

Mrs. Hirsch was quick to take me up on my offer and called me the very next day. "Actually, my kids—especially Shani—told me that they only want *you* to babysit for them!" she told me.

I smiled at the compliment. I must have done a good job the night before!

As the days wore on, I continued to babysit steadily for the Hirsches. The long hours I spent there were getting a bit overwhelming, especially because I had to balance that with my schoolwork and friends, too—but I just couldn't say no to the Hirsch kids. They really needed me.

"I have a strange request," Mrs. Hirsch said to me on the phone one afternoon. "I really need your help. We're having some trouble with my Shani."

That did not surprise me. Shani had been taking her father's illness the hardest of all of her siblings. She was often sad and out of it, frequently dissolving into a fit of tears for the smallest, most insignificant reasons.

"I'll be honest with you," Mrs. Hirsch continued.

"Her principal encouraged me to get her some help—and I mean professional help. Shani has been keeping her feelings to herself, bottled up inside, and it's not a good thing for her.

"At first she absolutely refused to see a social worker. She was embarrassed and scared. So I promised her that no one in her class would ever find out about it. I also promised her some big prizes, and she finally agreed to go. But it hasn't really been working out that well..."

"She may just need some more time," I pointed out.

"Of course," replied Mrs. Hirsch. "And we're not stopping the sessions with the social worker. However, she keeps telling me that she just wants to spend time with *you*. You're the only one she wants to talk to! My sister offered to take her out for pizza, but she said that she only wants to go with you. So, basically, I'm wondering if you have any extra time to give Shani these days..."

I was flattered. Indeed, Shani and I had always shared a special relationship, from the very first time I had babysat at her house.

Of course, I agreed to Mrs. Hirsch's request, and I took Shani out for ice cream that very afternoon. A few days later I took her out for pizza, and then, the next week, we went to the park together. As I became more and more of a "big sister" to Shani, Mrs. Hirsch asked Shani's therapist to give me some tools that I could use when dealing with Shani, to help her in an even greater capacity.

As I got ready to leave the Hirsch home one day, Mrs. Hirsch approached me, holding an envelope in her hand. "I have to tell you something, Mindy. You are making a bigger difference to Shani than anyone else is. I honestly don't know *what* I would do without you. I really don't know how I could thank you enough."

She slipped me the envelope, which contained a beautiful thank you card and a very generous gift certificate to one of my favorite stores.

Bouncing home afterwards, I felt like a million dollars. Wow! What a heady feeling! I was really making a difference in someone's life!

Sometimes, I underestimate my own abilities, I thought to myself, with more than a touch of pride. *I mean, look how much I've helped Shani Hirsch! If I could do that, I could conquer the world! I could do anything!*

I swung open the front door of my home. "Did you see my backpack anywhere?" I asked my younger sister Chani, who was sprawled on the couch. Now that I had conquered the world, it was time to tackle some schoolwork.

"Oh, so *now* you finally breeze into our house!" Her muffled reply came from deep down in the couch. "I thought you had moved in with the Hirsches!"

I rolled my eyes. "Listen, they really need me now."

Chani mumbled something under her breath.

"What was that?" I asked.

"Nothing," was her terse reply. She then stood up in a huff, walked to her room, and shut the door sharply behind her.

Wow! What was that all about? I wondered.

From the other side of Chani's bedroom door, I heard sobs. I sighed as comprehension dawned. I knew what this was about.

For months—since Chani had begun high school—I

had been in a state of semi-denial about her unhappiness there. While *I* loved every single aspect of my high school experience, my sister didn't seem to share those sentiments. She was not prepared for the intense workload that our high school demanded and was having a very difficult time with it. And the fact that all her good friends were attending a different high school didn't make things any better.

I felt bad for Chani—I really did—but what exactly was I supposed to do to remedy the situation? I was in eleventh grade, and she was in ninth. When I saw her around the hallways in school, of course I'd smile and talk to her for a few minutes, but that was about all I could do to lift her spirits.

Now, listening to her cries from outside her door, I realized just how miserable Chani really was. *If she's crying this way about it, things must have really gotten out of hand...*

I would have loved to make her feel better, but I had no idea what I could do for her. And I hadn't spoken to my best friend in days; I really had to catch up with her. *Go ahead—you may as well make the call now. There's nothing you could do for Chani anyway,* I told myself, trying to hush my burning conscience.

I retreated to my bedroom with the cordless phone and began punching the familiar numbers into it, but found myself hanging up before I hit the last digit. I sighed and walked back into the hallway. My sister was still sobbing.

I bit my lip. The ironic timing of my sister's meltdown, just moments after I'd taken care of Shani, was too much for me to miss. Here I was, making such a dramatic difference to little Shani, feeling like I could conquer the world and do anything—yet when it came to my own sister, I felt powerless and unable to help. How could that be?

The answer came to me in a jolt. Because my sister was my sister. When helping "others," like Shani, the issues were far removed and impersonal; they were "someone else's" problems. Yet, my sister's problems were so much closer to home; in fact, they *were* in my home. It gave me a sense of unease—and perhaps even embarrassment—to acknowledge that my sister had not found her place in high school. *How could someone in my own family be struggling like this?*

And, if I were to be brutally honest with myself, helping my sister was nowhere near as glorious as conquering the rest of the world. When I helped Shani Hirsch, I received gushy praise, appreciative words, letters, and gifts. Encouraging my sister, though, would not provide any of that.

And perhaps that's why helping Chani is an even bigger mitzvah, I thought as I knocked on my sister's door. I waited for her reply.

"What?" she finally asked between sobs.

"Can I come in?" I asked.

"What do you need?"

Inspiration hit. "I want to take you out for ice cream," I said.

There was no reply. I shrugged and walked back to my bedroom. *Can't say I didn't try to help my own sister.* Minutes later, I was engrossed in a heated conversation on the phone—and just then, my sister suddenly appeared.

"Okay, fine, let's go out for ice cream," she said.

This time, there was no Mrs. Hirsch slipping me cash to pay for the trip, and there were no elaborate words of thanks or praise. It was just me deciding to end the phone conversation with my friend, and then Chani and me heading out together to the ice cream parlor that I had become so familiar with over the past few weeks.

We chatted about this and that over our soft ice cream. My sister did not really discuss the struggles she was having in school, and I didn't probe her for information. When we left the place, I hadn't solved my sister's problems—but at least I had shown her that I cared, that I was there for her during this rough time.

It was a tough outing; in a way, it was more difficult than my outings with Shani. But I felt surprisingly good when we got home.

Because I had proven to myself that I *was* able to conquer the world, after all. Even my own world!

SECTION 4

Family Matters

Priceless

Hey Simi,
**School Shabbos is coming up. I totally
have nothing to wear! Think I could borrow
an outfit?**
Thanks a ton! U da best!

I read the note three times and then frowned. There
was no way I would give that note to Simi—no way in
the world.

Sifting through my closet the night before had been
depressing. I had set one mound of clothes as the "I
would *never* be caught wearing that" pile and then another pile as the "maybe" stash. But as I tried on outfits and the "maybes" quickly merged with the "I would
never wear that" pile, I realized that I'd have to come
up with something else—something new—to wear for
school Shabbos.

Really, it was pretty simple; I had to hit the mall. But when I had asked my mother if we could go shopping, she looked perturbed. She tried to reason with me that I really *did* have plenty of nice clothing, and I really did *not* need anything new.

But even as she spoke, I was able to tell that her heart was not there. Deep down, she knew that my wardrobe needed help, in the form of some new clothes. It's not like my mother's clueless; she actually has impeccable taste. Back in the good old days, when my father's jewelry business was booming, my mother and I went shopping all the time—in all of the finest stores in town.

That, however, was three years ago. And oh, how the times had changed. These days, my parents literally struggled to pay the bills and stay afloat. As for the extras in life, like new clothing, boots, or Chinese takeout? Forget about it!

So here I was, just a few days before school Shabbos (a.k.a. The Fashion Show—that's an unfortunate reality of life, at least in my school), with nothing decent to wear.

Asking my friend Simi if I could borrow an outfit had seemed like such a simple solution; she owned a ton—make that two tons—of stunning, expensive clothing. But I could never bring myself to ask her.

I crumpled up the note I'd written, and instead, I penned a new one.

Hi Sim!

So tired! I can hardly keep my eyes open!

Aw, school Shabbos is next week. What you wearing? You excited?

I glanced up at my teacher, who was writing

something on the board, and then flung the note onto Simi's desk.

I felt my face redden. I was too old to be passing notes to a friend in class. But I was desperate to know what Simi would be wearing to school Shabbos, and I simply couldn't wait for recess to find out. If I couldn't bring myself to ask her to lend me something from her closet, at least I had to know what my competition was in that area...

A minute later, Simi flicked a reply note back to me.

Yeah, me too, I could use a pillow, like NOW.

School Shabbos should be OK.

I'll wear whatever I pull out of my closet. Actually, I was thinking of stopping at Rachel's Fashions tonight.

I cringed when I saw the note. Rachel's Fashions was one of the most exclusive stores in town. Although my mother and I *used* to frequent that shop, I hadn't stepped foot in that store in over three years.

By the time I arrived home that afternoon, I was brimming with frustration. The messy kitchen (we could no longer afford cleaning help) only further soured my mood. I thought about the sorry state of my life. I hadn't been to camp in years, and we hadn't gone on a family vacation in recent history. My brother's bar mitzvah had been really simple—embarrassingly so, if you asked me—and now I couldn't even get new clothing! Life was tough. And unfair.

I'd have to talk to my parents about this.

When I walked into the dining room, where my parents were sitting, I knew the timing was all wrong. They were in the midst of sifting through a large pile of bills;

their facial expressions were rather grim.

"Ma, I really need some new clothing," I burst out, before I could think. My mother shot my father an exasperated look.

"Sweetheart," my mother said slowly, "I'm afraid that is not possible right now." She glanced at my father and then continued, "Actually, Tatty and I were just discussing the possibility of moving..."

"What?!"

"Yes," my father replied calmly. "To a smaller house, or maybe an apartment..."

Move? To an *apartment*? How terrible! How embarrassing!

I stomped to my bedroom and slammed the door. How would I ever explain this newest turn of events to my friends? They would never understand. As far as I could tell, their lives were all hunky-dory; they probably all thought that money grew on trees!

The large stack of clothing rejects, piled high on a chair in the corner of my room, added to my misery. From somewhere downstairs, I heard someone calling my name; apparently I had a phone call. I didn't want to talk to anyone, though, so I just ignored it. I sat down on my bed and dabbed my eyes with a tissue.

Fifteen minutes later, there was a knock on my bedroom door.

"I'm not available!" I called out.

My mother poked her head into my room. "It's me," she said. "I want to take you out. Are you available now?"

"Out?" I echoed. "To where?"

"I want to buy you a new Shabbos top," she said,

stepping into my room.

Our trip to T.J. Maxx was rather painful. My mother and I were used to shopping in exclusive shops and posh department stores, and now, here we were, combing T.J. Maxx's clearance racks for something decent.

And, lo and behold, I actually found something decent—even pretty—for ten dollars and ninety-nine cents! I arrived home in a slightly better mood; thankfully, I had something to wear. The future was still uncertain, but I'd worry about that another time.

My father tensed when I asked him for the school Shabbos fee.

"But—" I began to protest. I stopped abruptly when I saw the anxious look on his face. "Okay, I have an idea. I will use the Chanukah *gelt* I got from Bobby."

That was about the last thing I wanted to do with Bobby's Chanukah *gelt*. I was sure none of my cousins used *their* Chanukah *gelt* to pay for their school Shabbos trips. Yet, when my father warmly thanked me for my consideration, my resentment dwindled.

On the bus a few days later, I allowed myself to relax. Sure, I felt my stomach tighten a bit when Mindy showed up wearing a stunning pair of earrings, and when Simi told us about the new outfits she'd just purchased at Rachel's Fashions. For the most part, though, I had a nice ride up to the country.

The extended weekend passed in a whirl of activity, harmonized choirs, speeches and workshops, long DMCs, and too many midnight snacks. A couple of us overslept on Shabbos morning, and we scrambled to make it to the meal.

"Sim," I said, slipping on my Shabbos shoes, "we'd

better get going; it's really late. I don't know about you, but I am *so* not in the mood of making a grand entrance."

There was no answer, so I walked over to Simi, who was gazing into the full-length mirror. She tugged at the side of her skirt.

"This outfit is so ugly!" she burst out. "I don't know why I bought it!"

It was on the tip of my tongue to say, "Don't worry, the outfit is gorgeous." But I caught myself. I am an honest person; I wasn't going to say that.

"You look fine," I said instead. "Is this outfit new?"

"Yeah, don't ask," she said. "I just got it. I won't even tell you how much it cost! The saleslady said it's the latest style, and she convinced me to get it. I can't believe I listened to her! What a mistake!"

She finally walked away from the mirror, in a huff. "Yeah, I guess we better go."

We began walking toward the dining room. "*You*, on the other hand, look fantastic," Simi said to me. "Your sweater is stunning."

"Thank you." I smiled and accepted the compliment graciously. I neglected to mention that the beautiful sweater had come from the clearance rack in T.J. Maxx, and that it had cost me all of ten dollars and ninety-nine cents. *If only she knew!*

"You know," Simi continued, "you always know how to put yourself together so nicely, no matter what you wear."

By then, we had reached the dining room, and the noisy tumult that greeted us saved me from having to respond to that unexpected compliment.

But Simi's words lingered in my head for a long while afterwards.

On my way to the washing station, I caught a glimpse of myself in the mirror over the sink. I liked what I saw. It's true that my sweater—that amazing deal—was beautiful. But it was more than that.

I was beginning to realize that money is not everything, and that my parents' bank account did not have to define who I was. No matter how much or how little money we had, no matter how easy or how tough things were at home, I could still be the same beautiful, smart, and confident me.

And *that*, I knew, was truly priceless.

Miss Perfect's Sister

You know those perfect kinds of people? The ones who would look glamorous in pajamas and a messy bun? The kind of people who always know exactly what to say and how to say it? The ones who are adored by their teachers, classmates, and just about everyone else they come in contact with?

Well, that is *not* me! I am far from that kind of person. However, my older sister Chayala does happen to be a Miss Perfect.

The two of us have little in common. We certainly don't look alike, we don't act alike, and we don't think alike. Sometimes, I wonder how such different people were born to the same set of parents!

While I'm perpetually watching my weight, Chayala

is slim and trim without even trying. While my hair turns into a disastrous frizz-ball in the rain, for some mysterious reason, Chayala's hair always looks perfect. Always. She could get caught in a hailstorm, and then go swimming—and her hair would still look great.

When it comes to school, she is the one who shines. I, on the other hand, am a regular student. If I study, I do well; if I don't study, I don't do well. Chayala, on the other hand, does well regardless. And she's multi-talented, charismatic and kind, too.

So you may think I'm bitter and that I spend my life burning with jealousy. But I don't (usually) feel that way. I kind of enjoy my simple existence. And in any case, Chayala is so sweet that it's hard to be jealous of her.

But I admit, it is hard at times. Like when I get the inevitable *"You're* Chayala's sister?" question. As hard as I try not to, I do sometimes get a complex. How could I not? Especially when I entered high school; then Chayala's awesomeness and popularity really hit me in the face.

Like on Purim, when I spent the day watching a steady stream of Chayala's friends parade in and out of my home, each bearing a beautiful (and of course, themed) *mishloach manos* for her.

As for the parade of friends who came for me? Well, it didn't quite happen. Unless you consider the two friends who stopped by, plus the kids I babysit for, a parade.

At one point, I found myself gritting my teeth. *How on earth does Chayala have so many adoring friends?* I wondered. How is she so popular? Though, really, I shouldn't have wondered. I mean, she is Miss Perfect, after all, so the answer is really clear.

Finals time was also pretty difficult for me. Like most *regular* (as in "not perfect") girls out there, I went into a slight panic. Sure, I wasted time during my study sessions, but at least I was tense. At least I worried about my finals. Chayala, on the other hand, was cool as a cucumber and spent a large portion of her "wasting time" giggling and schmoozing with friends, and singing. (Yes, singing! Did I forget to mention that she has a fabulous voice?)

Again, I found myself gritting my teeth in frustration. It didn't make me feel any better when one of Chayala's numerous friends approached me and said, "You are so different from your older sister!"

"Gee, thanks for the compliment," I mumbled.

Chayala's friend just gave me a confused look and walked away.

So, as you can see, it sure isn't easy to be related to—let alone to live with—Miss Perfect. One day, however, my perspective changed. It was the day Chayala received her seminary replies.

For weeks, she and her friends had been talking about seminaries—harping over each little aspect of it and chewing over each option. Personally, I was sick of the topic and couldn't wait for them all to receive their replies and then fly off to Eretz Yisrael. Actually, the thought of a quiet home, without Chayala and her admirers, was kind of nice.

Chayala ended up applying to two seminaries. Her first choice was Machon Leah. That seminary was considered to be the "top seminary," and all of the "top girls" Chayala knew were planning to go there. Her second choice was Bnos Chaya. Now, there was nothing *wrong* with Bnos Chaya—it was a very good seminary, which attracted good Bais Yaakov girls—but it certainly didn't enjoy the prestige and status of Machon Leah. Chayala had only applied there because her teacher had insisted that the girls apply to two seminaries.

The acceptance (or rejection—but hey, that word could never be associated with Chayala) letters were expected to arrive one afternoon in mid-February.

"Ma, I'll call you at lunch to find out about the seminary replies," Chayala told our mother on her way out of the house that morning. Her voice was as chirpy as ever; it was evident that she was expecting an acceptance letter from Machon Leah. So much so, that she didn't even feel an element of suspense. I couldn't really blame her; I mean, which institution wouldn't roll out the red carpet for such a fabulous and talented young lady?

But on the bus ride home, when I asked Chayala to share the good news with me, she just shook her head. "It's so weird," she said. "I couldn't get through to Mommy today."

"Hmm...that is weird," I murmured.

As it turned out, though, my mother had intentionally missed Chayala's calls.

"Sweetheart," she said gently to Chayala, minutes after we'd burst through the front door, "I didn't want to tell you over the phone, while you were still in school. I thought it would be better to talk to you in person..."

A look of fear crossed my sister's face. "Uh-oh," she said. "What's the story?"

My mother did not have to answer the question. By

then, Chayala had walked over to the stack of mail on the counter and fingered the thin, small white envelope from the seminary of her dreams.

"Why such a thin letter?" she wondered aloud. She then read the letter and understood.

At first, she blinked, and reread the letter. Then her eyes drifted to the name on top. Perhaps it was a mistake. But no. The rejection letter was intended for her. She had been rejected from Machon Leah.

And let me tell you, the sight was not pretty. This sister of mine was not used to dealing with rejection. Chayala retreated to her bedroom, where she cried copious tears.

My mother tried to calm her down and reason with her. She tried to focus on the bright side. "But sweetheart," she said, "you *were* accepted into Bnos Chaya!"

That didn't quite cheer her up. It wasn't Bnos Chaya she had been pining to attend—it was Machon Leah.

As I stood outside Chayala's room, I actually felt bad for her. I contemplated going in to comfort my older sister. On the other hand, there wasn't much I could do for her. I mean, she had a gazillion friends who would no doubt be flying over, as soon as they heard the news, to make Chayala feel better; what did she need her little sis for?

Nonetheless, I knocked lightly on her door. When I received no reply, I took the liberty of walking in. Chayala's face was buried in her pillow. I glanced around and sat down awkwardly at her immaculate desk.

"Well," I said at last, "now we know that Machon Leah isn't such a great place after all."

I had piqued Chayala's curiosity. "Why is that?" I

heard the muffled response from her pillow.

"'Cause they have awful taste!" I replied indignantly. "They didn't take you!"

Despite herself, Chayala began giggling through her tears. It was pretty funny—she was kind of laughing and crying at the same time.

"If that's the case, I guess I don't even really want to go there anyway!" she said, and then giggled some more.

The giggles and sniffles gradually gave way to a comfortable sort of silence. Finally, Chayala sat up in bed.

"You're the best," she said. "You really made me feel better."

I walked out of my older sister's room with a smile. I had learned a couple of things from this whole incident: One, that nobody, not even my sister Chayala, is perfect or has a perfect life. And two, that everyone, even an almost-perfect person, needs some TLC from time to time...especially the kind of encouragement that only an ordinary little sister can give.

Vacation Blues

T-shirts: check. Sunblock: check. Sneakers: Check. I rummaged through my closet. Hmm...what else should I be packing for the three-day trip to Amish County and Hershey Park? Bored of packing, I plopped down on my bed, and picked up a book instead. *Hey, maybe I better take this book along,* I decided, and tossed it into my suitcase. As an afterthought, I tossed in a few more magazines. Better safe than sorry...

I was *so not* excited about this family trip! It was sure to be a real drag. I mean, Amish County? How boring! And Hershey Park? Big deal! That couldn't compare to the thrilling trip to Disneyland that my friend Esty would be taking.

So, the next morning, I'd be riding along in my

family's old, rickety minivan with my cranky siblings, while Esty would be flying off to California. And I'm sure that once she'd get there, in addition to visiting Disneyland, she'd be eating in elegant restaurants and going to other exciting attractions each day. And what exactly would *I* be doing? Oh, who knew exactly, but what I did know was that our family trip was sure to be one big, long bore...

It was pretty ironic. Just last week, I couldn't wait for my family's annual summer trip; we look forward to it practically all year. I was dreaming of the upside-down roller coasters in Hershey Park, the quirky games I'd play with my siblings in the car along the way, the barbecues and the "slumber party" at the hotel... Okay, so we would be staying in a pretty dumpy motel, and we wouldn't be visiting too many thrilling attractions. But still—family trips were fun, something I'd always looked forward to.

Until I bumped into Esty at a local pool one day.

"So, what are you doing these days?" she asked me, removing one headphone from an ear.

"Nothing much," I answered, putting down my swimming bag. "My family is actually going on vacation next week."

"Oh?" I had piqued Esty's curiosity; she removed her second headphone. "Where are you going?"

"We're going to Amish County and Hershey Park."

Was it the sun? Or was that a slight wrinkling of her nose?

"Amish County and Hershey Park?" She stifled a giggle. "I think I went there with my family when I was, like, five years old..."

I was quiet. It could be that Esty felt bad. "Hey, listen, I'm sure you'll have a nice time. It could be fun. I mean...I'm sure it can be lots of fun!" She put a bright—and fake—smile on her face.

"Actually," she continued, "I'm also going on vacation next week."

"That's nice," I mumbled. I was not enjoying the conversation at all. Something told me to walk away. To get away ASAP. But Esty was already chattering on, and I didn't know how to extricate myself from the situation.

"So I'm going with my sister and cousins," Esty continued. "We're going to California. I have an aunt there, and she is going to take us to Disneyland and to a bunch of other great attractions..."

"Sounds nice," I said again. Now I definitely wanted to get away from Esty. I chatted with her for another moment and then made my escape to the other side of the pool.

So, Esty was going to California. And I was going on a nerdy little road trip, with all of my siblings. Hmm.

That was why I wasn't terribly excited about the trip. I was therefore taking along plenty of reading material and anything else I could think of to keep myself occupied for the trip's duration.

From the next room, I heard my sister chatting on the phone, at about a million words a minute. She has a tendency to do that when she gets excited. I just rolled my eyes.

My younger brother traipsed into my room. He wanted to know if I had seen his kite.

Inwardly, I groaned. Come *on*! Were my siblings *really* going to be taking along kites? Kite-flying was *sooo* childish! I thought of my family flying kites. And then I thought of Esty and her cousins, prancing around all the "great attractions" in California! They'd be having the time of their lives, while I'd be getting a huge headache while listening to some kiddy music in the car (which, admittedly, was better than listening to my siblings' squabbles there) and refereeing fights (hey, someone's got to keep the peace in the back of the car!).

It was precisely with that attitude that I got into the car the next morning.

"We are going on *vacation,*" my father reminded me. "Not to a funeral. Did you mix it up? Is that why you look so miserable?"

"Yeah, why aren't you excited about our trip?" my mother asked.

Why wasn't I excited? Oh, it was too complicated to explain. I just shrugged my shoulders and mumbled something about being tired.

My father pulled out of the driveway. Uncle Moishy blared in the background. My brother wanted to know when we'd get there (and we weren't even on the highway yet!). My sister needed to stop for the bathroom, and yet another sister began kvetching that she was hungry.

It was going to be a *very* long car trip. The fact that my mind kept drifting off to Esty, who was probably boarding her flight just then, didn't help matters very much.

In the front of the car, my mother was fishing through the nosh bag, looking for a suitable snack for the hungry travelers.

"I didn't count on everyone getting hungry *already.*"

My mother laughed. "I think we'd better stop for some extra snacks."

"We're stopping? Already?" I blurted out. Visions of my family disembarking from the minivan and roaming the aisles of the local grocery—sporting Crocs, caps, and sunglasses—crossed my mind. Why, since everyone was already in vacation mode, they'd probably start flying their kites right there in the parking lot! And by then it would be supper time, and we'd probably pull out the grill and make a barbecue, right then and there, because everyone would be so hungry. Just for the record, we were located approximately two miles from my home. How utterly embarrassing!

We pulled into the parking lot of our local grocery store. I thought I saw my brother looking under his seat, where he'd stashed his kite. Yikes! I had to think quickly if I wanted to save face here.

"I have an idea!" I called out.

Everyone turned to look at me.

"How about if everyone waits in the car while I run in and grab what we need, and then we can get right back on the road?"

My mother shrugged. "Okay with me," she said. She gave me some money and told me which snacks to buy.

I ran into the grocery store and quickly scanned the aisles. I had to work fast; I didn't want my siblings traipsing in to see what was taking so long.

I was on line at the check-out when I bumped into my friend, Rivkah.

"Hey, where are you rushing off to?" she asked.

I blushed. "Oh, actually, I am on my way to Hershey Park."

"You serious?" she asked.

I laughed self-consciously. "Yeah, my family is waiting in the parking lot; we're going on a trip for a couple of days. I just ran in to get a few last-minute things that we needed..."

"Hershey Park?" Rivkah's eyes widened. "Wow. You are going to have a blast!"

"Yeah, I guess." I began to unload the snacks onto the conveyor belt.

"You are so lucky!" Rivkah said. "My family's idea of a great trip is to the local park. We've never even stayed in a hotel before."

Sheepishly, I looked up. Huh? I was the lucky one? That hadn't occurred to me!

By then, it was my turn to pay. I handed the money to the cashier, took my bags, and said goodbye to Rivkah.

I walked out of the store slowly, deep in thought—so deep in thought that I hardly noticed my brother roller-blading around the parking lot.

Wasn't *Esty* the lucky one? She was going to California, after all! But Rivkah thought *I* was lucky, because I was going with my family on a road trip. And yeah, she did sort of have a point: Hershey Park *is* a pretty fun place.

So maybe I *was* lucky. I just had to stop looking at others and what *they* had. And how lucky *they* were. And where *they* were going. Then I'd be able to see that maybe what I have isn't all that bad.

As we approached the highway, my father cracked a few jokes. I relaxed, and for the first time that day, I smiled.

The sun was shining, the collective mood in the car

was joyful, and no one was fighting. Yet. In a few hours, we'd be grilling some hamburgers at our motel. The next day, I'd be riding on an upside-down roller coaster with my siblings, and we'd alternate between laughing and shrieking our heads off.

I looked around the car. Come to think of it, I was a pretty lucky girl. It was all just a matter of perspective.

Of Parents and Pride

Great news!" my mother announced when I walked in from school one afternoon.

There was something about her tone of voice that told me I wouldn't think the news was as "great" as my mother thought it to be.

"What?" I asked, heading straight for the refrigerator. It had been a long day, and I *needed* a snack.

"Your school is making a women's tea," she said. "And they sent out a letter asking mothers to volunteer for the event."

I pulled some coleslaw out of the fridge, and paused. I didn't like what my mother was getting at.

"And now that Shimon's in playgroup, I have more time on my hands, so I decided to volunteer."

Oh, no, I moaned inwardly. Mommy? Volunteering for the women's tea? I could just see how well *that* would go over with my classmates.

"What did you volunteer to do?" I asked fearfully.

"I volunteered to coordinate the entire event!" she said with an enthusiastic smile. "I know that I never did anything like this before, and it will be a real challenge, but I figured it would be a great experience. And I might also enjoy it a lot!"

Disregarding the uncomfortable look on my face, Mommy continued, "Actually, I have a meeting at your school tomorrow at one o'clock. I'm going to be meeting with the other volunteers and the assistant principal. I went out this morning and bought some folders and memo pads to keep everything really organized. I figured I could—"

I was tired, and hungry, and I couldn't control myself any longer. "You're coming to *my* school? *Tomorrow*?" I blurted out. "At one o'clock? But that's lunch time!"

"And so?" My mother didn't understand the problem.

"But all my friends are going to be around! I mean— the whole school will be milling around at that time!"

"And?" Mommy still didn't seem to comprehend why I was so anxious.

I sighed. "What are you going to wear?" I asked in a small voice. Okay, maybe I was being a little rough on my mother, but if my *entire school* would be seeing her the next day, it was important—for my sake, anyway— that she at least "look right."

"Oh, please, I have no *clue* what I plan on wearing tomorrow!" My mother laughed. "Sweetheart, once you reach a certain age, you no longer put so much thought into these things... And in any case, I'll tell you what I *won't* be wearing: a name tag announcing that I am your mother! So you have nothing to worry about, Miriam."

As if no one would realize that Mommy's my mother...

I woke up the next morning with a vague sense of unease; I felt like it wasn't going to be a very good day. I dragged myself out of bed and began to listlessly pull on my uniform.

Suddenly, I stopped short. *That's what it is!* I remembered. *Mommy is coming to school today!*

"Oh, no!" I moaned.

"Is everything okay?" asked my younger sister, poking her head into my room.

"Yeah, everything's fine," I mumbled. She wouldn't get it. She was in seventh grade. There was no way she could understand the social pressures of a ninth grader.

It was about five minutes before my bus came that I ran to the pantry to grab something to eat.

"Good morning, sweetheart!" my mother greeted me.

"G'morning," I replied, grabbing a bag of chips and a chocolate bar.

"Is that all you're taking?" my mother asked. "Would you like me to make you a sandwich and bring it to you later on? I'll be in school anyway and—"

"NO thanks!" I answered before she even finished formulating her offer. "I mean, it's okay, Ma." I picked up a bag of whole wheat crackers. "See, I already found something to take with me. But thanks anyway."

My mother frowned. I wished her a good day and made my way to the door. She followed me.

"I'll see you later," she said.

"Ma," I said sheepishly, looking up at her, "is there any way you can wear your Shabbos *sheitel* to school today?"

"That again, Miriam?" My mother sighed. Then, catching sight of my pleading eyes, she said, "Okay, we'll see."

I felt a bit guilty about the way I had acted that morning, but I was too anxious to think much about it. I was hardly able to concentrate that entire morning; all I could think about was my mother's impending visit. I replayed dozens of possible scenarios in my head. Would my mother come over to me? Would she give me a...kiss? (Gasp!) Would she embarrass me in any other way?

Why, oh, why did she have to volunteer at *my* high school? I mean, there were dozens of other worthy organizations in town! And why did the meeting have to take place at precisely the moment when my entire grade would be milling around? I seriously felt a disaster brewing.

Ding, ding, ding.

My apprehensive thoughts were disturbed by the ringing of the bell. Most of my fellow classmates smiled. Ahh...finally, lunch time—a much-needed break after four long periods. It never arrived a moment too soon!

But I slumped in my seat. It was lunch time already? I limply pulled the package of whole wheat crackers out of my schoolbag. Next, I opened my loose-leaf and busied myself with "studying" as I chewed on my crackers. In all honesty, I did not have the head to "study"; I was actually seething inside.

"Hey, Miriam," said my friend Elky on her way out. "What happened to you? Suddenly, you're Miss Studious! Don't tell me that you're actually going to spend your lunch break *studying.*"

"No patience to go to the lunchroom today," I answered, hardly looking up from my notes.

"Okay, have fun with your notes," Elky snickered on her way out.

I was left on my own with my bland whole wheat crackers. Not a very pleasant lunch. At one point, I glanced at my watch. *Twenty minutes left till lunch is over. Then everyone will be back here, safe and sound, and Mommy will finish up her meeting and leave.*

But it wasn't so simple. Five minutes later, a few of my classmates came hurrying into the classroom with a shopping bag.

"Miriam! Guess who we saw!"

My heart sank. *No, this can't be happening!*

"Your mother!" Shani announced. "She was looking all over for you. She wanted to give *this* to you."

Shani placed the bag on my desk. There was a heavy scent of tuna emanating from the bag.

Why did Mommy do this to me?

Elky walked over to me. "Hey, is *that* why you hid out in the classroom over lunch time?" she teased. A few others looked at me, and my face turned beet red.

"Why *was* your mother in school today?" Shani asked. "She came to bring you your lunch?"

A few girls giggled, and my face reddened even more, if that was at all possible.

"No, she is working on the school tea," I answered, trying to sound as confident as I could.

The bell rang.

"Like a party planner?" asked Shani as she made her way to her seat. "That's cool."

A party planner? I liked how she put it. It *was* cool. But I was still embarrassed, more over the fact that I had hid from my mother and had been ashamed of her, than I had actually been over the fact that she came to school.

Yet, unfortunately, the situation went from bad to worse. Over the next few weeks, my mother constantly lingered around school. I feel bad to say this, but I was constantly embarrassed. Yes, of my mother. Of her outdated clothing, and less than perfect—and sometimes frizzy—*sheitel*. Of her sturdy and unstylish shoes, and of the way she greeted my classmates and teachers. (I mean, couldn't she be a little less conspicuous?)

Admittedly, she was working very hard, and from what I saw of her work, the tea promised to be a beautiful event. I was too wrapped up in my own mortification, though, to take much notice.

Did my worst nightmare come true—that my mother would ruin my social status among my friends in school? Well, thankfully not. But I was on edge for the entire few weeks that my mother was around the school while she worked on the event.

The morning after the tea, my teacher walked into the classroom and immediately searched me out. "Miriam, I must tell you: your mother did a fantastic job!" she announced out loud, in front of the entire class. "Last night's tea was the most beautiful one the school has ever had! The theme and color scheme were absolutely brilliant! You must be so proud of your mother."

And suddenly, I did feel a surge of pride. My class-mates looked over in my direction, but this time I didn't blush; I smiled. So my mother was not the queen of fashion, nor did she own the snazziest wardrobe in town. But she had so much else going for her. She was creative! She was talented! She was a good party plan-ner—and that certainly *was* something impressive.

Years have passed since my mother organized that tea when I was in ninth grade. And throughout high school, I had plenty of embarrassing moments. Like the time my father came to pick me up from school and sent my little sister inside to find me. Or the time my mother came backstage after one of the concerts, to take some pictures of me with my friends. Or the awk-ward comments my parents sometimes made when my friends came over.

But I learned to hold my head up high anyway. This is my family. These are my parents. And they are great people.

Are they the most typical people in town? No. Is my mother the most stylish and "with-it" lady around? Not at all. Do they sometimes make comments that slightly embarrass their children? It does happen from time to time. (And they are not the only parents who do that!)

But they are wonderful and kind people, nonethe-less. I am proud of them for who they are. And I am proud of myself, for having gained the maturity that allows me to accept and take pride in my wonderful parents.

My Little Sis

*K*nock, knock.

I let out a deep sigh. This was the fourth time that my little sister, Rikki, was knocking on my bedroom door. Why was she bothering me so much tonight? Didn't she realize that we had a murderous history midterm to study for? And didn't she know that I had four friends over?

Actually, that was precisely the reason *why* she kept finding her way into my bedroom. See, Rikki is in eighth grade, and I am in tenth grade. And for some reason, Rikki thinks that tenth grade high school girls are the coolest people on the planet.

"What is it, Rikki?" I asked, swinging my bedroom door open yet again.

Rikki was holding a math book. "Do any of you re-member how to do the Pythagorean Theorem?" She looked around hopefully.

Oh, come on! The Pythagorean Theorem? We were up to important things! (Okay, really we were in the middle of a heated discussion about the school concert, but I didn't have to tell her that.)

"Rikki," I said, trying my best to sound patient (I didn't want my friends to think I was a mean sister!), "we are in middle of studying, and we really don't—"

My friend, Leah, interrupted me. "Actually, I can help you with that," she said, taking the math book. "It's not even that hard. Here, let me show you..."

Rikki had a smug look on her face as she settled on the plush carpet in my bedroom. I cringed. Here my friends and I were, studying—okay, not studying, but having a great time—and Rikki kept on barging in, bothering us, and completely ruining things!

Pythagorean Theorem, my foot! That was just an ex-cuse; somehow Rikki managed to hang around us for the next hour. I was fuming. When my friends left, I stormed into the kitchen.

"Ma!" I said. "Can you tell Rikki that she *has* to stay away from my friends when they come over?!"

"Chani, calm down," my mother said. "What's going on?"

"My friends came over to study for our history mid-term, and we could hardly get in a word of studying because Rikki kept on bothering us!"

By then, Rikki had entered the kitchen, too. "That's not true," she said. "I only came in a couple of times, when I had a question with my homework!"

"How come you only have questions with your homework when my friends come over?" I pointed out.

She blushed. "It's not like that! I just..."

"Chani, sweetheart," my mother said to me, "you have to understand that you and Rikki are the only girls in a family full of boys... She needs you. And yes, she wants to feel a part of things when there are girls around. That is not unreasonable."

Of course, Ma took Rikki's side. I was in a rotten mood, and hardly managed to finish studying for my midterm. By the time I got into bed, it was past two. I lay tossing and turning, thinking about my evening.

That's it, I decided. *I can't have friends over anymore. All of our get-togethers will have to happen elsewhere.*

This was a real shame, because my house had always been "Grand Central Station." My mother is very accommodating and always has great food around, and I have my own spacious bedroom. But too bad; no more partying near Rikki, because she managed to get on my nerves every time my friends came over. So we'd have to party (I mean study) elsewhere.

When my friends approached me a couple of days later and asked to come over and study, I knew I had to think fast. *We can't get together in my house,* I thought. *There is just no way...*

"I have a great idea!" I said to them. "How about studying at the park? We can bring our notes, find a nice shady spot at the lake, and we're set!"

My friends loved the idea. I called my mother to ask if she could drive us over, and to my delight, she agreed.

"I'll be happy to drive you girls over...but there is

one condition. I want Rikki and her friend to come along, too. They are also studying for a test, and once I'm driving out to the park, why not let them have a chance to enjoy some fresh air?"

"But Ma!" I protested. "It is... I can't... I mean—"

Ma cut me off. "You *can*. Rikki is your sister, and I want you to be nice to her and make her and her friend feel welcome."

I was so frustrated. Here I was, trying to run away from Rikki, and instead she was about to ruin our afternoon at the park! But I had no choice. Unless she and her friend tagged along, there was no way we were going.

Rikki, of course, was elated to join our exclusive trip to the park, as was her friend. During the car ride, they chattered and giggled. I cringed. Little sisters could be soooo annoying! Couldn't Rikki just pipe down for a minute? And give *me* a chance to get in a few words?

Apparently not. Rikki was convinced that an entire minivan of high school girls was interested in hearing about her high school entrance exams.

I finally cut Rikki off and changed the topic. I felt a bit guilty when I saw the disappointed look that crossed her face. But hey, these were *my* friends. And we weren't obligated to talk about *her* topics... Right? I tried to convince myself.

Admittedly, the afternoon at the park was actually a lot of fun. Of course, it would have been a whole lot *more* fun without Rikki. But there are some things in life that are not in my control.

Like the sweater episode...

The following Motza'ei Shabbos, my grade was

having a *melaveh malkah,* and I planned on wearing my new gray cardigan.

I went to my closet, but it wasn't there. *That's weird,* I thought. *I was sure it was here...* The phone rang. It was my friend Leah; she would be picking me up in about ten minutes. The frantic search continued.

I looked through my closet again, and then went to the laundry room. There wasn't a trace of my cardigan. I contemplated wearing something else, but that cardigan looked so good on me... As a last resort, I ran over to Rikki's room—and lo and behold! There was *my* stunning new cardigan—in *her* hamper.

How could she do this to me? I fumed.

I had to settle with wearing something else, and I was unhappy about the way I looked that whole night. It was all Rikki's fault that I didn't enjoy the *melaveh malkah.*

"How could you do that?" I asked Rikki later that night. "How could you borrow my favorite sweater without asking for permission?"

"Sorry, Chani, I didn't think you would mind. I only wore it for a couple of hours on Shabbos when I went to visit my friend."

I was furious. Why did Rikki always ruin things for me? Little sisters were so annoying and difficult...

Later that night, I told Ma what happened.

"Chani," she said, "you are right. She should not have borrowed your cardigan without permission. But don't you think you are getting carried away? Rikki is not ruining your life. *You* are making *yourself* miserable by blowing things out of proportion. So you didn't have your gray cardigan. If I recall correctly, you own the very same cardigan in black. And wearing a black sweater instead of a gray one to a grade *melaveh malkah* should not ruin the evening for you. The only thing that can ruin it for you is your own attitude."

I sighed. I understood what Ma was saying. But on the other hand, she just didn't understand how difficult it was to have a little sister. Especially one like Rikki.

"Chani, yes, sometimes little sisters can be a bit annoying. They like to tag along, and they sometimes borrow items without permission..."

I nodded vigorously.

My mother smiled. "Those things are not in your control. They happen, and trust me, I did the same to my older sisters when I was little! But what *is* in your control is the way you react. You don't have to let this ruin your life."

I just grunted.

"And one more thing, Chani," Ma added. "I want you to know that sisters are the biggest gifts in life. Friends come and friends go, but sisters are your best friends forever. Trust me: one day, you will appreciate Rikki."

Rikki? Best friends with me? Ha! What a thought!

But a few weeks later, I understood, just a bit, what Ma had said. I had a terrible stomach virus. It was 4:00 a.m. and I couldn't sleep. I lay in bed, feeling miserable and groaning.

Suddenly, Rikki appeared. "Chan, are you okay?" she asked.

"No! I feel miserable!" I managed. "My stomach is killing, and I am *sooo* nauseous."

"*Oy*, I'm sorry to hear that."

Before I even had to ask, she went downstairs and

returned a few minutes later with a steaming cup of tea for me. Suddenly, her presence was not so annoying. Then she went down to bring me some crackers. She sat and schmoozed with me for the next hour and a half, distracting me from my pain, until I felt somewhat better.

"I think I'm going back to sleep now," I said sleepily, picking up my covers.

"Okay, feel good," Rikki said and walked back to her own room.

At 4:00 a.m., when all of my friends were deep in sleep, it was my little sister who was there for me. I thought about what my mother had said. *Friends come and friends go, but sisters are your best friends forever.* Best friends—now maybe that was pushing it; but still, maybe it wasn't so bad to have a little sis, after all.

A Link in the Chain

The day of my family's annual Thanksgiving dinner, on the fourth Thursday of November, was fast approaching.

The very thought of this annual family dinner made me cringe. I mean, which normal Bais Yaakov girl attends a Thanksgiving dinner? But unfortunately for me, my extended family has a large Thanksgiving dinner event each year which I am expected (or rather *forced*) to attend.

The grand dinner event always takes place in my home. The reason my mother hosts it each year is because she is the only member of her extended family that keeps kosher. Yup, my mother—and for that matter, my father, too—are both *baalei teshuvah*; they became *frum* later on in life. I therefore have no *frum* grandparents or cousins.

How does this affect my daily life? It really doesn't. My parents are just like all of my friends' parents. My father learns *Daf Yomi* each morning and is quite proficient in halachah. My mother loves attending *shiurim* and listening to Torah lectures on her MP3 player; she is also quite knowledgeable in halachah, and in Tanach as well. My mother wears a pretty *sheitel* and stylish but *tzniusdik* clothing, and really doesn't look any different from your typical *frum*-from-birth woman.

My relatives, on the other hand, do not look anything like my friends' relatives. And that is actually a gross understatement! My relatives are *very* different from my family. Some of my relatives respect our choices and lifestyle; some don't. Either way, we try not to discuss religious topics and Bais Yaakov/yeshivah education with them; instead we stick to safer ground (like weather and traffic).

I recall one of the most embarrassing moments in my childhood: the day my aunt showed up to one of my elementary school productions, wearing pants! I thought I would faint.

I tried to pretend that I didn't know who my aunt was, that she was some distant relative I had never seen before (I figured I could always give her her due attention later on). But Auntie Betty walked right up to me and embraced me like I was one of her dearest nieces (which I actually was). She also planted a large kiss right in the center of my forehead. And she was wearing Hot. Pink. Lipstick.

"I am so proud of my niece!" she said, beaming, to my teacher, who politely smiled back.

I was so ashamed and miserable that whole night that I was hardly able to sleep. I was sure that my social status was permanently ruined. But thankfully, the next day, my life continued as usual, and—wonder of wonders—my friends still talked to me. Hardly any of my classmates even mentioned my aunt. What a relief that was!

But even aside from the awkward and embarrassing moments like these, caused by my family situation, throughout my childhood I've always felt a deep sense of loneliness. There were so many times when I wished I had cousins to hang out with and grandparents to spend Shabbos and Yom Tov *seudos* with. Unfortunately, though, I never did. The only meals shared with extended family were those Thanksgiving family dinners, which I would have happily done without!

As Thanksgiving approached this year, I tried to suggest that instead of serving turkey, we should serve steak—or even chicken cutlets—at the family dinner. But my mother said that turkey was a "traditional food" and all of the relatives expected it—so there was no choice about that.

Dinner began with an in-depth description of my Auntie Martha's sewing classes and a subsequent art show. She pulled out her phone and showed us pictures of the quilts she was working on. We then got to hear all about the bake sale that she hosted for her son's preschool.

Then, Uncle Bertie spoke up. "Did I tell you about Nettie's surgery?" he asked. Just for the record, Nettie is a dog. But we all listened politely as he discussed the dog's surgery, subsequent recovery period, and kind vet.

Afterwards, one of my cousins engaged us in a captivating description of the grand extracurricular activities offered at her high school. From the way she made it sound, it seemed like they never actually learned real subjects there! After she finished describing the new horse her school had just bought, my cousin Terry turned to me and asked, "So, what kind of extracurricular activities does *your* school have?"

Well, we certainly don't have any horses, I thought with a smirk. I took a long sip of Coke as I tried to think of what to answer.

"Well, my high school puts on a concert each year," I finally said. *And please, please, please don't ask me about it! Because you totally won't get it!*

No such luck. "Tell me all about it!" said Terry.

"Well, I was in song-dance last year." I smiled. "Um... it was a lot of fun!"

"Song-dance?" she asked. "I don't get it. Is that like a song? Or a dance?" She giggled. To her, the term 'song-dance' was as ludicrous as horses in high school!

We were on such different wavelengths; our lives were as different as night and day. We just didn't get each other. Needless to say, that family get-together was just as painful and as dreary an experience for me as always.

To make matters worse, the timing of these "grand" parties, for some reason, usually coincided with my own social events. For example, the night of the Thanksgiving party this year was the same night as my friend's birthday party at a local café. But of course, there was no way in the world my mother would ever let me miss the Thanksgiving dinner...

Fast-forward a month. We were back in our dining room, this time for my family's annual Chanukah party. And this time, it was only us: my parents, my siblings, and me. My mother had tried her best to create a festive atmosphere; she had bought funky Chanukah paper goods with menorahs imprinted on them, custard donuts, crispy latkes, and a new Chanukah CD. She had also bought presents for all of us and a few artsy dreidels. But though she tried very hard to make a nice party, none of her efforts were able to compensate for the greatest factor missing from the party: the people. At the end of the day, it's the guests that make the party, and that's something we did not have at ours.

Before long, my older sister retreated to her bedroom to call a friend. My brother ran out to his *rebbi's* Chanukah *mesibah* (which he claimed would be a *real* Chanukah party). I was left to clean up the messy dining room.

The room was just about spotless when my father walked in. "Thank you so much for cleaning up," he said as he settled down beside his menorah. He gazed at the dancing flames. "They're still going strong," he noted with satisfaction. "Great wicks this year!"

I remained quiet. *I'm glad the wicks are making my father happy—but I feel a terrible void in my heart.*

"Is everything okay?" asked my father, glancing up.

"It's just so unfair!" I burst out.

My father looked startled. "What's unfair?" he asked.

I hesitated for a moment as I contemplated how—and

if—I should express myself. I felt bad; it wasn't my father's fault that his parents and siblings weren't *frum*!

"Didn't you enjoy the Chanukah party tonight?" asked my father.

No! I totally didn't, I thought to myself. *Tomorrow, I'm going hear about the hall that my friend Gitty's grandparents rented for their massive family Chanukah party. I am going to hear all about the one-man band they had, what each* balabuste *in the family prepared for the party, and the performance that all of her cousins made. Compared to that, our party was dull, nerdy, and downright pitiful.* But I couldn't say this to my father, who was looking at me expectantly.

"It was nice... I mean, really it was! It's just that...." I paused for a moment, and then it all came pouring out. "It's just that we have no one to celebrate with! I mean, it was just our family! It was so quiet and depressing. All of my friends have parties each and every night with different sets of cousins, grandparents, and relatives. And *our* family? We have one nerdy Chanukah party—with just us!"

I grabbed a blue Chanukah-themed napkin from the dining room table and dabbed my eyes. "All of my friends have cousins, aunts, uncles, family *simchos*, and parties. I feel so...so left out! So isolated!"

I reached for another napkin, trying mightily to stop the tears that were streaming down my face. "Sorry," I whispered. "I didn't mean to lose myself like this..."

My father was quiet for a moment. Then he said softly, "It seems that certain times during the year are harder than others."

I nodded.

Another pause. "There really isn't much I can do for you, honey," my father said. "I understand that it is hard; I wish I could make it up to you in some way. I know that our cozy little party tonight wasn't as grand as your friends' family parties..."

Again I nodded.

"But I want to tell you something important, Esty," he continued. "You are a link in the chain. You are creating the next generation in Klal Yisrael. *Your* children will, *b'ezras Hashem*, have *frum* grandparents and *frum* cousins."

Hmm. I hadn't thought about that. That was certainly a nice thought...

"Give it some time; give it a few years. You'll see. With Hashem's help, it won't be too long before our home becomes filled with grandchildren, and then our parties will be a lot more—"

"Happening," I finished for him. "And happy!"

We both grinned.

I would hang in there. No, it wasn't always easy, but it was a *nisayon* that I would have to make peace with.

And if I ever did become down about not having *frum* relatives, well, I could always think of my grandchildren attending a large family Chanukah party one day—with lots of *frum* relatives—and that would make me smile...

The In-House Babysitter

I am counting down the days until Pesach vacation!" my friend Mimi gushed one evening as we chatted on the phone. "I could *so* use the break!"

Pesach? Break? I thought to myself. *How could those two words be uttered in the same sentence?*

I tried changing the topic, but no such luck. Mimi droned on and on about all that she hoped to do over Pesach vacation. Her plans included shopping excursions, socializing with friends, going to the pool...oh, and helping her mother, too, for good measure.

"And then comes Yom Tov itself, which is always so relaxing and beautiful!" Mimi finished.

I quickly excused myself and hung up in a huff. It's not like Mimi had said anything wrong per se; she had just struck a very sensitive chord in me. To me, the description of Yom Tov as a relaxing and beautiful vacation was almost comical! "Chaotic" would be a better word to describe Yom Tov in my home.

Mimi would never get it, though. She lives in a picture-perfect home. You know, the kind where the floor seems to clean itself. (Or maybe their live-in housekeeper is the one who keeps it sparkling clean.) There is always a moist Bundt cake in a domed cake stand on the kitchen counter, and starched outfits on matching hangers lined up in the closets.

My home just isn't like that; it never was, and it never will be—and especially not on Yom Tov! I'm the youngest of nine, and all of my older siblings are married. I have lots of nieces and nephews, *bli ayin hara*. My siblings and their families love coming to us for Yom Tov, because, as they all say, "Mommy is so amazingly easygoing."

Well, my mother *is* easygoing, even over Yom Tov—but I have to say, I'm sure it's partly because she knows she has *my* help! So the pre-Yom Tov—and especially pre-Pesach—season never leaves me with much time to hang out and relax. There are always mountains of potatoes to peel, apples to core, and beds to make. But truthfully, it's not the pre-Pesach cleaning and cooking that gets to me. It's the babysitting—the constant, never-ending babysitting of my nieces and nephews.

Don't get me wrong: I love all of my nieces and nephews dearly! It is just the extended babysitting sessions that I don't enjoy. As they say, too much of a good thing is not always such a good thing...

A day before Pesach, my mother asked me to gather my belongings and take them out of my room. "I am going to put a couple in your bedroom," she told me matter-of-factly.

"But I don't *want* to give up my room!" I burst out.

My mother was taken aback. Sure, in the past, I had graciously volunteered to give up my bedroom for Yom Tov—but you know what? I was getting older, and it was no longer so easy! I needed space! And privacy! Sleeping on a cot in the corner of a bedroom with all of my nieces and nephews did not really provide peace, quiet, or privacy.

My mother looked so exhausted and overwhelmed that I immediately felt bad about my outburst. "It's okay," I quickly mumbled. "I'll manage without my room for a week."

But that didn't mean I was doing this happily. I stalked off to my bedroom and closed the door behind me. *I DO NOT WANT to give up my space and turn into a homeless (or rather bedroom-less) girl for Yom Tov!* I thought bitterly to myself. But it didn't seem that I had much of a choice...

Adding insult to injury was the phone call I received from Mimi later that afternoon.

"Temima, are you up for a quick dip in my aunt's pool?"

I almost burst out laughing. Swimming? The day before Pesach? I felt like Mimi was living on some other planet!

You can understand, then, why I was a bit cold and stiff when my married siblings and all of their kids began to arrive on Erev Yom Tov.

My mother was full of smiles. There were *sheitel* boxes, suitcases, diaper bags, jackets, and potato chip bags scattered all over the living room and kitchen, but that hardly fazed her. On the other hand, the messy house really did irk me!

Why can't they all keep track of their stuff? I wondered. I thought about Mimi and her family, who were probably taking their Erev Pesach naps right now in their quiet and spotless home, and a scowl crossed my face.

"Hey, Temima! Are you okay?" My brother broke into my thoughts.

"Yeah, I'm great," I said crisply.

"Could have fooled me!" he said heartily as he headed back to his minivan for another load of stuff.

There was no time (or place) for me to take a nap that afternoon. My usually quiet and orderly home had turned into a chaotic mess. Kids, toys, ices, candy, socks, and shoes were all over the place.

When I went to get dressed on the first day of Yom Tov, I noticed that some of my possessions, such as my new belt and my favorite black skirt, had mysteriously disappeared.

"Kids!" I called to my nieces and nephews. "Whoever finds my stuff will get a big prize!"

Thankfully, the skirt and belt turned up shortly afterwards...in a junk pile in the kids' room. I was not amused.

Needless to say, I was not a very happy camper that day. When my sister asked me to babysit her kids so she could take a "quick nap," I almost exploded! Sure, I realized that my sister was tired. But honestly, so was I!

I couldn't believe I was saying yes to my sis—but of course I did. I felt bad to refuse her request; it seemed easier to babysit her kids than to turn her down.

"My kids all love spending time with you," my sister was quick to point out before retreating to her (that is, *my*) bedroom.

As if that would sweeten my mood at all.

It turned out that her "quick nap" was not that "quick," after all. I did have some time to lie down afterwards, but my house was too noisy and I was too frustrated to fall asleep.

This situation repeated itself day after day. By the time the second days of Yom Tov rolled around, I felt like a worn-out *shmatte*; I was grouchy and tired. Was this what *simchas Yom Tov* was all about? The worst part was the resentment that I felt toward my married siblings. That made me feel horrible.

"Temima! Can you take us to the park?" my niece asked me on the last day of Pesach.

"Yeah, what a great idea!" her mother—my sister—chimed in, with a broad smile. Of course she thought it was a great idea; that would mean some peace and quiet for her! I, however, did *not* think it was a great idea.

Hot tears sprang from my eyes. I felt so used! The whole Yom Tov I'd been helping, giving, doing for my family, for everyone else... Didn't anyone realize how badly *I* needed some time for *myself*? And some space and privacy? I was so tired, and I so badly needed a break!

My sister was genuinely surprised by my tears, and I felt silly for crying.

"Sorry, it's just...I've had a difficult Yom Tov...I think I need a break this afternoon," I whimpered.

"No problem," said my sister. "I'm glad you said so. I'll take the kids to the park."

At last, I was a free bird! I quickly got dressed and headed out to visit Mimi, where I was sure I'd have some peace and quiet. As I walked to her house, I had time to reflect on my Yom Tov experience.

I've been so taken advantage of! The aggravating thought crashed through my mind. *How could my siblings have left to take naps or to go to shul while I stayed and watched their children? How do they have the nerve to ask me to babysit so many times?*

I quickened my pace, while continuing to stew in my anger. *Yeah, I love kids, and I am thrilled to have my nieces and nephews over, but I wasn't even able to enjoy them over Yom Tov because of how hard their parents made me work!*

"How could they *do* that to me?" I mumbled aloud. Slightly embarrassed, I glanced over my shoulder to make sure no one had heard me. Sheesh! Was I actually talking to myself? That meant I was *really* upset.

And then suddenly, the answer to my question hit me like a ton of bricks. It was actually quite simple: My siblings asked me to babysit for them so many times *because I never told them no*!

This realization was quite humbling, because it meant that, in a way, I was at fault for the way I was feeling. I had the choice; no one was forcing me to babysit or make myself into a *shmatte*. I could be assertive and express my needs clearly—and people would understand and respect me for that (as my older sister had just done). Yes, as long as I was polite and nice about it, I *could* sometimes say no!

I only wished I had come to this realization earlier. Now it was already the last day of Pesach, and so much of my Yom Tov had already been filled with anger, hurt, and resentment...

By this point, I had reached Mimi's home. We sat in her gleaming kitchen as her housekeeper served us seltzer and Pesach cake. The quiet was so absolutely delightful. Apparently, though, Mimi felt otherwise.

"My Yom Tov was so boring," she said with a scowl. She took a long sip of seltzer from her crystal stemmed glass and then continued, "I wish we had whom to invite over for Yom Tov. You are so lucky to have so many guests."

"Are you *serious*?" I asked, shocked. Mimi nodded.

All I could do was laugh. I guess the grass *is* always greener on the other side!

SECTION 5

Life Is a Test

Life with ADHD

What in the world was my teacher talking about? It was the first week of seventh grade. I was sitting in class, staring blankly at my teacher, Miss Stein, who was talking in Japanese, at about a million words per minute. I looked down at my Chumash and desperately began flipping the pages. Feeling totally lost, I glanced at Baila, the girl beside me, to try to catch a glimpse of the right place.

"Faigy, we're in *perek chaf daled, pasuk yud,*" Miss Stein announced.

My page-flipping became more frantic. *What did Miss Stein say, perek yud, pasak* what?

"Faigy, we're learning *Navi* now, not Chumash!" Baila whispered with a smirk.

"Oh." As I slipped my Chumash back into my desk, I felt my face redden. By then, Miss Stein was already deep into the lesson. I officially gave up; I didn't even bother taking out my *Navi*. In any case, I realized, I'd left my *Navi* at home.

At first, I tried to sit still and listen to the lesson, sans my *sefer*, but it soon got *very* boring. I opened my pencil case and began fiddling with my white-out. Then, I took apart my new pen.

"Faigy, are you with us?" asked Miss Stein.

"Um...can I go to the bathroom?"

By the time Miss Stein gave me permission to leave the classroom, I was already out the door. I walked quickly in the direction of the bathroom, but truthfully, I would have been happy to go anywhere; I just needed to escape from the classroom.

In reality, Miss Stein had not been talking Japanese. But to me, it sounded that way, because I have a very hard time focusing and am very often feeling hyper. You see, I have ADHD (Attention Deficit Hyperactivity Disorder), and back then, my condition had not yet been treated. This made it virtually impossible for me to sit through class.

I really *did* want to be a good student and keep up with my class. I honestly did *not* want to cause trouble. Each day, right before class began, I'd say to myself, "Today I will focus and listen to my teachers. I will do everything perfectly."

But then, I'd see a bird outside the classroom window, which would remind me of the time my family went to Six Flags and saw a great exhibit with all sorts of rare birds. My mind would continue down that path and I'd think about my favorite ride in Six Flags—the Mind Train Roller Coaster. Oh, how my sister and I had shrieked our heads off when we got to the big drop at the end of it...

Then I'd suddenly notice twenty-six sets of eyes focusing on me and Miss Stein asking, "So, Faigy, do you know the answer?"

I'd understand that Miss Stein must have just asked me a question, but how should I know the correct answer when my mind was so many miles away, still perched on the top of the big drop of the Mind Train?

Usually, before I'd even realize it, the words, "amusement park!" or something of that sort would roll off my tongue. Then, the class would roar with laughter, and the teacher would glare at me and ask to see me after class.

Then, she'd turn to another girl for the answer to her question, while I'd be left fighting back tears of frustration, wondering where I'd gone wrong.

I'm a smart girl. Why didn't I pay attention to Miss Stein? Then I could have answered her question perfectly, and she would have praised me instead of given me a punishment... When I got dressed this morning, I was sure that today would be perfect, that I would be an A+ student in class... How did things sour so quickly?

But at that point in my life, being an A+ student was not a feasible goal. Not because I didn't want to be one, and not because I wasn't smart. It was impossible for me to live up to my potential because I wasn't receiving the proper help to treat my ADHD.

I am grateful that those days are now behind me, and I try to block those painful memories from my mind. Since I have begun receiving help, my life is considerably easier—though it is still not a bed of roses.

Once a month, I see a psychiatrist, who prescribes medication for me. I need to take the medication once a day, and it helps me stay focused and pay attention. It also makes me less hyper, though nothing can completely eradicate my hyper tendencies. When I forget to take my medication, my day is sure to be a disaster.

I don't enjoy taking the medication, because it ruins my appetite and it can also make me dizzy at times. But I know that taking the medicine is a whole lot better than the alternative, and so I really try to be conscientious about taking it each day.

As a teenager, I am a bit embarrassed about the fact that I see a psychiatrist. But I keep it private, so none of my friends know about it, and I also try to remind myself that seeing a psychiatrist is nothing to be ashamed of. Lots of people have medical conditions and see doctors for all sorts of things, all the time. For my condition, ADHD, I see a doctor, too—only it's a different kind of doctor than an ordinary physician.

I also make sure that all my teachers are informed of the fact that I have ADHD, so that they can understand me—and my behavior—better. I want them to know that with the right help, I can be a great student; I can shine! I try to always choose a seat in the front of the classroom, because I know from experience that it's a lot easier for me to concentrate sitting in the front of the room than in the back. And whenever I start to feel jumpy sitting in class, I take the liberty of leaving the room for a few minutes to air out (now that my teachers are familiar with my condition and my needs, I have their full permission to do this whenever I feel it's necessary).

ADHD doesn't only manifest itself in a school setting. Living with ADHD means trying to fight my natural restlessness all the time; whether while doing homework in my room, while doing my best not to annoy my siblings with my often hyperactive behavior, and while trying to fall asleep at night despite my constantly racing mind.

With all the challenges my ADHD brings, I know that it is not my fault that I was born with this condition. I also know that ADHD comes along with a tremendously positive side, as well—for instance, my creativity and the energy I have which allows me to accomplish so much.

Living with ADHD is not easy, but with the help and support of my parents—and of course, Hashem—I am doing my best to live my life to its fullest. And you know what? I am a very happy person.

My First Kitchen Encounter

It began with an innocent invitation.

"Malky," my friend Tzippy said on our way home from school on a Friday afternoon, "my brothers are away for Shabbos. Why don't you join us for *shalosh seudos*?"

It sounded like a nice idea, and I readily accepted her invitation.

And that is when the trouble began. What can be so troublesome about a meal at a friend's house? The cheesecake.

The meal itself was rather uneventful. Then, the cheesecake came out for dessert; it was one of the most delectable and divine cheesecakes I have ever tasted. I had to hold myself back from taking triples.

"Wow, where'd you buy this from?" I asked Tzippy.

"*Buy*? *Cheesecake*?" The idea seemed ludicrous to her. "Never! I actually made it."

I gaped at her. This beautiful and delicious cheesecake was made, created, and baked by Tzippy herself? Apparently, though, she didn't think it was such a big deal. For the next couple of minutes, she regaled me with all the things that she regularly baked and cooked. I remained quiet, having nothing to add. What could I tell her? That I knew how to make frozen pizza?

I went home that evening with a complex—a rather large one. And I wondered: was I the only teen out there who wouldn't recognize a frying pan if it hit me in the face? I tried to convince myself that there were lots of teens—and even women—out there who were completely clueless when it came to cooking. Still, when Tzippy came to school a few days later with some awesome chocolate chip cookies that she had "thrown into the oven at twelve o'clock last night," I couldn't shake the feeling of inadequacy that came over me.

Especially when a few other girls began discussing recipes, too.

I was amazed at how many of my friends knew how to cook. And I was determined to join their ranks, too.

So when my mother mentioned that she'd have to stay late at work on Wednesday evening, I jumped at the golden opportunity.

"I'll make dinner!" I offered.

My mother was taken aback. "*You'll* make *dinner*? But you've never cooked before!"

"It doesn't matter," I said stubbornly. "I know how to follow directions. I'll find some good recipes and follow them to the tee, and"—I snapped my fingers—"you'll have supper made by the time you get home, just like that."

My mother was still reluctant about it, but she agreed to let me try. "As long as you clean up the kitchen afterwards!" she made sure to stipulate.

And so, on Monday evening, I set out to plan the menu. I curled into bed with a couple of cookbooks and flipped through the glossy pages. Wow. There were so many choices, and the pictures all looked mouthwatering. Narrowing my dinner down to a couple of dishes would not be easy.

Finally, I settled on a recipe called pan-seared duck with lingo berry for the main dish. It looked absolutely divine, at least in the photo. But then, as I scanned through the ingredient list, I frowned as I realized that I hadn't the foggiest clue what a lingo berry was, or, for that matter, if it even grew on this side of the planet! So in the end, I settled on glazed chicken bottoms. Not as fancy as pan-seared duck with lingo berry, but definitely more doable.

When I came home from school on Wednesday, I immediately settled myself in the kitchen. Donning my mother's apron, I gathered all the necessary ingredients and began cooking. First, I made the chicken. Next, I cooked a pasta dish to accompany it. For an added treat, I decided to make some chewy brownies to go with my dinner.

In all honesty, I did not find my first cooking session to be as glamorous as my cheesecake-baking friend made it sound. I was hot and overwhelmed, the kitchen was a royal wreck, and I had splattered guck all over my mother's cookbooks. But it was invigorating, and, as I cleaned up the mess I had made, I smiled, thinking of my family enjoying my home-cooked dinner while I basked in the compliments. Of course, I'd try to be modest and shrug off the compliments, sort of like Tzippy had done; I'd make it sound like it was no big deal... Or maybe I wouldn't; after all, I had worked hard and I did deserve the compliments!

To make a long story short, there weren't too many compliments forthcoming that evening.

I did, however, learn a thing or two about cooking:

1. A teaspoon of baking powder is not replaceable with a tablespoon of baking powder.
2. A *bulb* of garlic should not be mistaken for a *clove* of garlic.
3. The bake time at the end of a recipe is not a suggestion. It is a command.
4. When cooking pasta, the water should be placed in the pot *before* the pasta. And it should be boiling by the time you put the pasta in.

Needless to say, I was rather dejected about my cooking fiasco. It was evident that cooking and baking were not my forte.

I considered my grim future: I'd be the only wife and mother in town who couldn't cook and wouldn't know a tablespoon from a ladle. The others would pursue the latest recipes and discuss their grand menus, while I'd be sticking takeout in the microwave. My poor family would have to live off of takeout food, bakery challah, and frozen pizza, because I didn't know how to cook. Why, I wouldn't even need a kitchen in my future home, because I'd hardly have a use for it! And for that matter…would anyone even *want* to marry me, a girl who didn't know how to cook?

Yikes! The thought was scary!

So it was official: I was a complete and utter failure—in the culinary department, at least. There was no hope. And, for that matter, what *was* I good at?

I headed off to school the next morning in a pretty lousy mood.

The piece of paper I found on my desk just added salt to my wounds.

"It's the cheesecake recipe that you asked for," said Tzippy.

I picked it up cautiously and glanced through it. *You so* wish *I could pull this off,* I thought. I quickly stuffed the recipe into the bottom of my schoolbag, planning to throw it in the garbage at the next available opportunity.

When my teacher began the lesson, I was unable to concentrate, so I began doodling in the margins of my notebook. Well, there: I may not have been the world's best cook, but I knew how to draw! I was not a failure in life! I also had a pretty decent voice, and I did pretty well in school; those talents did count for something—didn't they?

Yeah, right. I thought of a *shadchan* telling someone that, "she can't cook, but she knows how to draw! And sing!" That sure didn't sound too great to me.

Not wanting to wallow in these disturbing thoughts, I tried to move on and think of happier thoughts instead. *You'll worry about* shidduchim *and your poor culinary skills when you get closer to* shidduchim *age,* I told myself. *And until then, you'll simply avoid the kitchen like the plague.*

But my mother had other plans. We were having company for Shabbos that week, and she wanted me to make the chicken and some brownies.

I just stared at her. Was she kidding? She wanted *me* back in the kitchen? It wasn't enough that I had trashed it the other day, made a mess of her new cookbook, and then served a tasteless and unappetizing meal to everyone? Did she really want a repeat performance of all that?!

But apparently, she wasn't joking.

"You said you realized the mistakes you made last time," she replied, "so now you need to try it again, making sure *not* to repeat those mistakes *this* time."

My first thought was: *NO WAY.*

But then my mother began telling me about all the horror stories that had happened to her when *she* started cooking. "Listen, it happens to the best of us," she said. "Messing up is part of the learning process…"

I didn't have much to lose, so I tentatively re-entered the kitchen. Wiping aside the food stains from the cookbook, I carefully—very carefully—read the recipe. I was a lot less confident this time—and a lot more cautious.

The pan of brownies went into the oven. I waited with bated breath until it was ready to come out. Then I let it cool on the counter, just as the recipe said. The brownies really looked good, so I took a tiny taste…and it was actually delicious!

Soon the chicken came out of the oven, and it, too, smelled pretty great.

I couldn't believe it. Had I really made these delicious foods myself? Was I really able to cook, after all?

Just then, my sister walked into the kitchen.

"Here, taste these brownies," I said to her. "They're yum!"

"Um...it's okay. I mean, I'm sure they're amazing and all, but...I'm not really in the mood of brownies right now..."

"Stop it," I told her. "You're just scared that they taste like my first batch of brownies. But they don't! These brownies really are delicious!"

I cut a piece of the brownie and gave it to her. She took a tiny nibble, and then a big bite.

"You're right!" she said, around a mouthful of cake. "This is great! *You* made these brownies?"

Yes, *I* had made them. And it hadn't even been that hard. All it had taken was a bit of perseverance—and a mother who wouldn't allow me to give up so easily.

As my sister helped herself to a second brownie, I smiled. Then I ran off in search of my schoolbag. I hoped that I hadn't yet thrown out the cheesecake recipe from Tzippy. I planned to make that cheesecake one of these days.

Because I'd seen firsthand that, with enough patience and persistence, I could do anything—even in the kitchen!

Breaking Free

Peer pressure. I learned what that meant when I entered high school. And it just increased as the months passed...

It was the end of ninth grade, and I was filled with pre-camp jitters. I wanted to do everything right. I wanted to have a perfect summer. I want to fit in so, so badly. Those were the thoughts and wishes that consumed me as I shopped for camp clothes with my mother.

"These shirts are nice, Temima," my mother said, walking over to a large display of colored shirts.

I sighed. Yes, technically the shirts were fine. But those weren't the ones I wanted; I wanted the ones that all my friends would be wearing. I wanted to be part of the "in" crowd. But how would I explain that to my mother?

"They're okay, I guess," I said. But then I pointed to the shirts I really wanted, on display at the other side of the store. "But I like these so much better."

Now, it was my mother who sighed—when she glanced at the price tag. The shirts I wanted were triple the price of the shirts she had picked out!

In the end, we compromised and got a few of each. My mother wasn't thrilled about getting any of the expensive shirts, but seeing that this was important to me and being that the expensive shirts were completely *tzniusdik*, too, she (thankfully!) decided not make a big deal about it.

I hardly slept the night before camp was to begin; I was terribly nervous. On the first day of camp, I dressed carefully, blow-drying my hair until each strand was styled properly and making sure the sweatshirt I flung over my shirt sported a "J" on the zipper. I looked just right. I hoped.

As I surveyed myself in the mirror, my conscience piped up, *Since when do you care about brand names? Last summer you couldn't care less...* How had I gotten swept into the peer pressure? How had I become a follower of the latest trends?

But the peer pressure did not stop with my clothing. Shortly after camp, I decided that I needed a cell phone. All my camp friends had cell phones, and if I didn't have one, there was no way in the world I'd be able to keep up with them! Why, I was practically the last girl on the planet without her own phone; at least that's how I felt.

But there was a problem: my parents were not such big fans of all the modern technology out there, and they did not believe in teenagers having their own cell phones. In fact, my mother had only recently gotten a phone for herself!

Still, I decided it didn't hurt to ask, and so, one night after supper, I carefully broached the subject to my mother.

My mother's response was just what I'd expected it to be: "I'm sorry, Temima, but I really don't see a need for you to have a cell phone."

"It would be to keep in touch with my friends!" I answered.

"But we have two landlines. Why can't you keep in touch with your friends using the regular phones? Why do you have to talk to them on a cell phone?"

I sighed. "The lines are always busy. And my friends can never get through to me at home! They can't call late at night. Anyway, *no one* really uses house phones anymore! And when I'm away from the house, no one has any way of reaching me."

I paused, suddenly realizing how ridiculous that last argument sounded—who was I, already? A tenth grader. Why did I have to be so accessible? But I simply wanted a cell phone so badly. I didn't want to be the only "nerd" without a phone of her own.

My mother told me that she would think about it and discuss it with my father.

In the end, my parents reluctantly gave in. I think it was the fact that "all the other parents let" that clinched it; they didn't want me to be the only "different" girl, either.

How excited I was when I first got my phone! It

was such an exhilarating feeling—I was finally "part of things!" I spent that entire evening playing with my sleek new toy and admiring all of its wonderful features. *Wow, these things are awesome!* I thought. *I don't know how they managed without them in the olden days.*

I stayed up in bed until a very late hour that night, texting my camp friends.

At some point, my conscience began bothering me. It reminded me of how the principal in my school had spoken out against texting, and that technically, we weren't supposed to have texting on our phones. Or maybe not? *Was* there a rule against texting? I couldn't remember exactly.

But in any case, it really doesn't matter, I comforted myself. *What matters is what I actually do with the texting. And asking my camp friend about her school Shabbos, and passing on a joke to my married sister, are both quite harmless.*

With that, I quieted my conscience. Even if there was a school rule against texting, it surely was not meant for girls like me, girls who would never do anything wrong with their texting.

And indeed, I didn't do anything wrong with my texting—unless wasting time is counted as doing something wrong, of course. Things continued in this way, and I enjoyed my cell phone—including the texting feature—for the next six months.

One day, I went to a *shiur* with my older sister. The speaker, a prominent *rav*, was speaking about the dangers of technology. Since my family did not have Internet access in our home, I mentally patted myself on the back, feeling good.

He's not talking to me, I thought smugly. *For once, I am doing everything right! Nothing to feel guilty about!* And I allowed myself to tune out.

I felt my fingers itching towards my cell phone, which was in my pocket, but I controlled myself. It would be really rude to text in the middle of a speech, even if the speech didn't apply to me.

But suddenly, I heard the *rav* say something about texting. Without my even realizing it, my ears perked up, and I tuned back into the speech.

The *rav* was sharing a story. It was about a good, *frum* Bais Yaakov girl, who, like me, had texting on her phone. A few texts to the wrong people...and that was the beginning of a terrible downward slide for this girl. And it all began with a few simple text messages.

I glanced down at the bulging pocket of my jacket, where my cell phone lay. *But this wouldn't happen to me,* I tried to soothe myself.

"It's a scary world out there!" the *rav* thundered. "There are so many *nisyonos,* and the *yetzer hara* is so strong..."

I couldn't get the story out of my head. And later that night, as I lay in my bed, a scary thought suddenly crossed my mind: *The girl from the* rav's *story could have thought the same exact thing as I am thinking right now, that "this could never happen to me"...*

Oh, my. Did that mean I was just as vulnerable as this girl?!

The flash of clarity I had propelled me to make a sudden decision, one that I am so grateful I made. I went downstairs to the kitchen, where my parents were still up and talking to each other. I asked my parents if they could please call Verizon and tell them to block the texting ability from my phone.

"Wow, Temima, that is very special," my mother said in an awed voice.

My father looked up from the paper he was reading. "Temima...we're very proud of you."

I went to sleep feeling good about myself.

This feeling did not last for long, though. By the very next morning, I began to second-guess my decision. *What was I thinking? I am going to be so "out of things" without being able to text!*

My friends did not make me feel any better.

"Hey, Temima," said my friend Rikki the following day. "Why didn't you answer me? I sent you three text messages last night."

My face turned red. "Um..." I stammered. Well, I'd have to tell everyone what I had done. I couldn't exactly hide it; my friends had to know why I wasn't answering their messages. "I blocked texting from my phone." I tried to sound confident.

"You what?" questioned Rikki.

"Blocked texting," I explained patiently. "I can no longer receive any text messages, and I can't send any either."

"Is your phone broken?" Rikki wanted to know. By then, a few others had joined the conversation.

I sighed. Here it came. "No, I had Verizon take it off my phone. I don't want to have texting on my phone anymore."

An animated discussion followed.

"But come on," Rikki said above the crowd. "When they say those types of things and all those stories about the *yetzer hara* of texting, they don't mean girls like *us!*"

I tried to explain what the *rav* had said: that it's a scary world out there, and that no one can ever trust themselves, as the *yetzer hara* is so strong.

"Still," huffed Rikki as she walked away, "I think you are being a *bit* extreme."

It wasn't easy. Without my texting ability, I *was* somewhat out of things. I missed out on some invitations, and I wasn't in on some of the latest jokes. There was the time a friend was trying on gowns for her brother's wedding and wanted to send me a picture message so I could share my opinion on which one I liked best. But I wasn't able to receive messages, and so I couldn't see the gowns. And there were lots of other instances like this...

At times like these, I wanted to give in to the *yetzer hara* and put texting back on my phone. But each time, I held strong. And I began to feel very good about my decision. I was doing the right thing.

With time, my friends began to respect me for what I had done. But really, that was not the point; that wasn't most important. What *was* important was that I respected myself for this decision I had made. And nothing felt better than that.

In the Know

How did high school differ from elementary school?

There were plenty of ways. One noticeable difference was the *hock* and stories that went around in high school.

In elementary school, life was fairly simple. Sure, we all had our friends, and exciting events did take place from time to time. Occasionally, an interesting story would come up. But other than that, school life was pretty uneventful.

So when I noticed a cluster of girls huddled together on one of the first days of high school, I curiously approached them. They were talking in excited voices, and I felt like I *had* to know what was going on.

"What's up?" I asked, trying my best to sound nonchalant.

"You didn't hear?" Dena replied.

"Hear what?" I questioned.

"About Rivka's cell phone."

"Big deal," I said. "Lots of girls have cell phones."

"No, but she was *caught!*" Dena said triumphantly. "And it was confiscated!" She continued to fill me in on all the details. Apparently, a teacher had caught Rivka talking on her phone outside the school building, and it seemed that she was in deep trouble. But I didn't get it. Why were the girls so *excited* about this story?

"I mean, this is major news!" Dena explained.

Okay, I guess it was. I stuck around for another few minutes as we discussed "The Thrilling Cell Phone Confiscation Saga," until the bell rang.

"Hey, what was that about?" my friend Hadassah whispered to me as we settled into our seats.

I gave her a knowing smile. "Long story—I'll tell you later," I whispered back.

And tell her I did that evening, in great detail.

"Wow, you really have a grip on the goings-on in school!" Hadassah commented.

I smiled. I'll admit: it did feel good to be "in the know."

As the weeks progressed, other stories cropped up. Unlike elementary school, high school was always full of action. Things *happened* in high school. And girls—specifically teenage girls—like to talk. So there were always clusters of girls ready and eager to analyze each episode that occurred in school. Sure, technically speaking, there were lots of more important things to talk about other than ninth grade politics and high school *hock*. But to us ninth graders, these were the most important subjects in the world!

"Did you hear about the ninth grade *melaveh malkah*?" Malka, a popular girl in the class, asked a group of attentive listeners one afternoon. I quickly joined the audience.

"No, what's the story?" I asked.

"There is a new rule this year!" Malka paused for a dramatic effect. Satisfied by our intense curiosity, she continued, "It's a long story how I found out. I'm sure they will tell us soon, but basically, this year, they are going to make us wear our *uniforms* to the *melaveh malkah!*"

"No way!" someone exclaimed. "Our u*niforms*?!"

Inwardly, I was relieved; it sure removed some of the pressure of the upcoming event. But I had to pretend I was disappointed. "But come on, it's Motza'ei Shabbos! How on earth can they force us to wear uniforms then? It makes no sense."

"Beats me!" Malka shrugged. "Maybe they don't really trust us. Maybe our teachers are scared that the whole *melaveh malkah* will turn into a fashion show."

Her last statement sparked another heated discussion, which lasted until the bell rang and we had to go to class.

When my friend Esty called me later that day to ask something about the Chumash quiz, I jumped at the opportunity to share the sizzling hot *hock* with someone who did not yet know it.

I told her, in great detail, about the school making us wear our uniforms to the *melaveh malkah*, perhaps even taking the liberty to throw in some of my own (possibly true) commentary to the news flash.

I finished my rant and paused—but I received no reaction from Esty. I felt like an actress on stage with no audience.

"Hello?" I asked. "Are you still there?"

"Um, yeah," answered Esty. "I'm just a little busy here. What were you saying? You got a new uniform skirt?"

Huh? She had totally missed the point.

"Oh, nothing," I grumbled. "What did you want to know about the quiz?"

I answered her question and hung up. If she couldn't care less about the latest ninth grade *hock*, that was fine with me; I'd simply find another friend, a girl who *would* be an eager listener, to share the tidbit with.

The *melaveh malkah* came and went. Despite the fact that we had to wear our uniforms, it was a lovely affair. And with the *hock* about that having gone stale, a new piece of news soon came up, and I once again found myself in a huddle of excited girls.

"I heard that they are thinking of cancelling the school concert!" announced Malka one morning.

"*What?!*" we all shrieked.

"How can they do that?" I protested. We all began talking at once.

"Okay," Malka finally admitted, "they aren't exactly going to *cancel* it; they are thinking of making it a bi-yearly event, meaning there would only be a concert every other year."

This particular rumor that Malka had so confidently shared with the rest of us turned out to be just that—a rumor. However, I soon learned that rumors, true facts, fiction, and stories oftentimes swirl together into a blend of information for all those up on the latest news...

Things continued in this way for a while, with me constantly running after the latest *hock*. I just *had* to know everything. There were those girls who didn't really care about what was going on and spent their recess and free time talking about irrelevant and boring topics. I, however, prided myself on being "in the know." I loved when friends and classmates called me up to ask questions about something that was going on. It felt so good to be people's source of information, to know exactly what was happening and when.

Leaving school one afternoon, I felt a bit frustrated. It seemed that a juicy piece of news had gone straight over my head. I had heard that Elky, one of my friends in the parallel class, was suspended from school for a day for some reason or other, but I was having a hard time finding out about the details.

I felt a pang because Elky was supposedly one of my good friends. Why hadn't she shared anything with me? Did that mean that she didn't value my friendship? I tried calling her that evening, but my phone calls went unanswered. Double pang. Next, I tried my friend Esty.

"What's going on with Elky?" I asked her. Elky sat right in front of her in class; surely, Esty would know what had happened with her.

To my chagrin, however, she didn't.

"I don't know anything about it, and honestly, I really couldn't care less!" Esty said.

I was aghast. "It doesn't bother you to be so out of things?"

Esty snorted. "All this *hock* is just a bunch of silly nonsense. I miss one story today; by next week, it's history. Why should I waste my time with a bunch of fleeting squabbles and things like that?"

"But still," I persisted. "Aren't you curious?"

"Nah," she replied. "I just let these things slide off me. I'd rather spend my time talking about intelligent and meaningful things instead."

I just shook my head. "Whatever," I replied. In eighth grade, I had felt like Esty and I understood each other so well. Oh, how the times had changed.

"Also," Esty added, "has it ever occurred to you that these 'stories' and 'rumors' might be *lashon hara*?"

At that, I couldn't keep the sarcastic retort from jumping off my lips. "Oh, so now this is turning into a *mussar schmooze,* huh?"

Esty was silent for a moment. Then, in a very soft voice, she said, "And one more thing: why would people want to share a personal piece of information with someone who talks so much? How could they trust her?"

Now, it was my turn to be silent. Could that be why Elky was avoiding me?

Suddenly feeling very uncomfortable, I wished Esty a quick good night, and the awkward conversation ended.

So I never did quite find out what the suspension in the parallel class had been all about. However, after a painful episode the next day, I no longer cared to know about it.

It was lunch time, and I had to go to the office to make some photocopies. As I walked down the hall on

my way back to the classroom, I heard a few girls talking to each other. Curious, I quickened my pace. And
then, as I entered the classroom, they were suddenly
quiet.

"Hey, what's going on?" I asked.

Silence. No one answered my question. I saw two
girls glance at each other with uncomfortable expressions on their faces.

"Nothing much," someone finally replied. She then
quickly changed the topic.

The truth sank in. *They must have been talking about
me.*

I turned around and quickly walked out of the classroom. In a daze, I met up with Esty.

"Is everything okay?" she asked, taking in my strick-
en face.

"Um, no, but..." I paused. "I thought about what you
said last night. You are so right. It is not important to be
in on every silly story that crops up. As you said, it can
lead to *lashon hara,* which is so destructive..."

"I'm glad you finally realize it," she replied with a
smile.

Suddenly, I didn't feel so distant from Esty anymore.
We could still understand each other, after all. We sat
down to eat lunch together.

"I read the most fascinating article in a magazine
last night," Esty told me. "Want to hear about it?"

"Sure!" I said, and I really meant it. What a welcome
change, to hear about something substantial and real,
instead of just some more fluffy gossip.

Still, when the next exciting tidbit of information
came up, later that afternoon, I found myself burning

with curiosity. I wanted nothing more than to dive in and hear each and every juicy detail about what was going on...

But I paused, remembering my hurt from earlier that day. And I realized that joining this conversation would very likely lead to speaking *lashon hara.*

Just walk away and let this story slide off of you, like Esty does, I told myself.

But...to miss out on this exciting piece of *hock*...? I couldn't do that...I just *had* to know what was going on...

I hesitated for another moment—and then I walked away.

I smiled. I *could* do it. It might not be easy for me. Each day and each juicy story would present a new challenge, I knew. But I *could* rise above it and keep away from all that *hock* and *lashon hara.* I *could* do it.

Public Property

C'mon, Riva, cheer up!" said Gila one afternoon over lunch. "Last I checked the world hasn't come to an end. Not yet, at least."

The others around us smiled at her attempt at humor; I, however, did not find it very funny. For that matter, I didn't think *anything* was funny these days.

"For real, Riva," Gila continued. "You look *so* down these days. Are you feeling okay?"

"Mmm... Yeah, I'm feeling great," I said in a distracted voice.

"Really? You could have fooled me. Try to smile; it won't hurt you..."

I walked away, annoyed. Easy for her to say. Her life was all nice and dandy; it was no wonder Gila always walked around with such a winning smile.

My life, on the other hand.... Well, let's just put it this way: it was far from being easy and far from being happy. At least, as of recently.

My father had come down with a terrible infection in his leg. I wasn't sure about the details, and quite frankly, I didn't want to know them, because I found the whole thing to be scary. All I knew was that my father was admitted to the hospital, and I heard someone mention something about the danger of "losing a leg" if it wasn't properly cared for.

On top of that, my grandfather—my mother's father—had not been well recently, so my mother was running back and forth between my father and her own father.

And there was more: Recently, my brother, who was "in *shidduchim*," had met a great girl. Since I knew her from camp, I was over the moon with excitement about the match. She was a really cute girl, with the most awesome personality. Everyone in camp—including myself—really liked her.

The *shidduch* seemed to have been progressing nicely, and I was already dreaming of the engagement, of calling all my camp friends with the thrilling news, and of beautiful gowns.

And then, quite abruptly, it came to an end.

Of course, I knew better than to ask my brother about it directly, and my mother wasn't being too forthcoming with information for me. But really, the whys and the hows didn't matter; the point was, it was over. They were not getting engaged. No thrilling news to share, no parties to attend, and no gowns to wear. And it wasn't even like I could share this disappointment with friends to gain their sympathy.

It was all enough to put any girl in a lousy mood.

So that is why I was sitting over my soggy cream cheese sandwich and moping. Sure, I knew that was wrong. I mean, of course it's not nice to mope around and greet my friends with a grouchy face. But who could blame me? Life was tough.

Once I got into the "I'm in a bad mood, and it's too bad, nothing can change me, so deal with it" rut, it was hard to get out. Somehow, it felt easier to frown, grumble, slump in my seat, and do my own thing than to pull myself together and try to smile. So, while all the girls sat outside during lunch, enjoying the nice weather, I found a comfortable seat inside—alone. While they went for a walk during the free period, I stayed in an empty classroom and caught up on some math homework.

I'm not sure at exactly which point it hit me, but I finally realized how isolated I was. While my phone used to ring off the hook, it was suddenly eerily silent. I'd go out for a couple of hours and return home to no missed calls at all. No one stopped by to visit on Shabbos anymore, and in general, it seemed like my friends were avoiding me.

What had gotten into my friends? So I was not in the greatest mood these days, and perhaps I had not been the world's best company, but hey, was that a reason to avoid me? Because of my bad mood, my friends should have specifically gone out of their way to be *extra* nice to me.

When I bumped into Gila, I decided to confront her

about it. "Gila, what's with you these days?" I asked.

"What's with *me*?" she responded. "The better question would be: what's with *you* these days?"

"With me? Same old. But what I meant to ask you was why you've been avoiding me."

Gila looked surprised. "Why? Because... Well, because it seemed like you *wanted* to be alone," she answered.

"Why did you think that?" I asked in a small voice. "You thought that I didn't need my friends anymore?"

"Well, yeah," answered Gila. "Haven't you noticed that whenever the girls get together for lunch or something, you always choose to stay by yourself? So...we all figured...you wanted to be left alone."

I was silent.

"And to tell you the truth," Gila continued, "you've been in a pretty grumpy mood for a long while, and, well, no offense, but...you know, no one likes to hang out with a grouch who spends the entire day frowning."

At this, I felt my frustration level rising. Sure, Gila was the happiest person around. Her constant smile, kind words, funny comments, and infectious giggle defined her. So, yeah, we all liked to hang around Gila. But who was *she* to talk to *me* about smiling and being in a good mood?! The nerve of her! She was only a happy person *because* she had a perfect life! It wasn't like I'd chosen to have these *nisyonos* and be in a bad mood!

Noting the dark expression on my face, Gila quickly apologized. "Sorry, I didn't mean to hurt you. I was just trying to give you some friendly advice."

"Thanks, but no thanks," I said. "It is all very lovely for you to tell me to 'be happy.' I guarantee you, that if my life was as perfect and happy as yours, I'd walk around with a smile the size of New Jersey."

For a split second, I saw a gray cloud hover over Gila's happy demeanor and her smile quivered. She opened her mouth as if to say something, but quickly shut it and remained quiet.

After a moment of silence, she finally said, "Riva, I want to talk to you."

Some more friendly advice? I thought. I'd had enough of that from her, thank you very much!

"What is it?" I asked warily.

She glanced around. "Not here, not now. Do you want to walk me home from school today? We'll talk then."

"Okay," I agreed. "I'll meet you after school." No one would be home that evening, so I didn't have anything to run home for.

As soon as the final bell rang, I met Gila outside. Throughout our walk home, we made small talk. We chatted about the weather, school Shabbos, hairstyles, and her nieces and nephews. We were walking onto her block when I realized that she had yet to begin her "talk"—the whole reason we had walked home together. I was beginning to get curious about it, but I decided not to ask her. I didn't want to be a nudge, and in any case, I was sure she would tell me sooner or later.

When we arrived at Gila's front door, she paused for a minute and fished through her bag until she found a key. She slowly opened the door and flicked on a light switch.

"I'm thirsty," she said, leading me inside. "Can I get you something to eat or—" She suddenly paused when we reached the kitchen.

"Oh, my, I'm so embarrassed," she apologized. "I can't believe it. My brothers left such a mess!"

"Don't worry about it," I said, taking a seat at the island in the center of the kitchen. "I've seen worse."

Gila smiled. "Are you sure?"

"Certain!" I smiled back.

"Well, let me tell you why this house is flying," she said, placing a bottle of orange juice and two cups beside us. "Actually, this is exactly what I wanted to discuss with you."

I was confused. A moment later, though, I understood.

"I am a pretty closed person," Gila began, "so none of my friends know this...but my mother is...sick. That is why she's not around, and there's no one to really take care of the house."

"I am sorry to hear that," I stammered. What else could I say?

Fortunately, Gila went right on talking. "Sometimes she *is* home, but even then she is too weak to do anything around the house. It's been really tough..."

We spent the next half hour commiserating with each other. I was able to understand exactly what she was going through, as my family life was also pretty crazy these days.

Suddenly, I remembered our talk from earlier that day. "Wait! But with all this going on, how can you still be so happy?"

She smiled. "That's exactly why I decided to share this information with you now. Remember when you said to me that if only your life was as perfect as mine, *then* you'd be happy?"

I blushed. "I'm so sorry. When I said that, I didn't realize..."

"Nothing to be sorry about!" was Gila's hearty reply. "How were you to know my family situation? But when you said that to me, I couldn't keep my secret in any longer. So I decided to talk to you. For my sake, to unload. And for your sake, because I wanted to show you that happiness is not contingent on external factors like what is going on in your life."

"Huh?"

"Let me explain with a pillow." Gila ran off to her bedroom to retrieve something. She returned a moment later with a cute decorative pillow. On it was written a quote: "Happiness is not a destination. It is a journey."

"My mother bought this for me," she explained. "And I think of this quote often. Happiness—true happiness—is not a destination. You will never arrive at the happiness point in life—a point where you will say, 'Now I can be happy.' Basically, you've just got to make yourself happy, no matter which point you're at or what's going on in your life..."

"Yeah, but even when things are so difficult, like they are now for both of us?" I asked.

"Yes," she answered, "because if you're not happy now, who knows if you ever will be happy?"

"But—"

"Look at me," Gila interrupted. "I have every reason to be miserable, wouldn't you agree? But I choose to be happy anyway, because if I choose to be sad, you know who will suffer most from that decision? Me.

"And," Gila continued quietly, "everyone else will suffer, too. Your face is public property, you know. If you decide to frown and be a grump, those around you see it and automatically feel grumpy, too. And it's just not fair to do that to someone."

I sighed.

"Listen," Gila said. "It isn't easy, but you've just got to try to make yourself happy, despite the rough things going on in your life. Trust me: in the long run, it's worth it."

And I did trust her—because she'd been there, done that.

I walked home from Gila's house slowly; I had a lot to think about. When I arrived home, I noticed my mother's minivan in the driveway. Hey, she was home.

"Hi, Ma!" I called out as I flung open the front door.

"I'm over here!" I heard the muffled reply from the laundry room.

I walked over to greet her. "How was your day?" I asked.

"Okay..." Her head was deep in a laundry bin. She looked up and saw my bright face. "Hey, what's the good news?"

"Oh, nothing in particular," I replied. "It never hurts to smile..."

My mother blinked, and then returned my smile with a dazzling one of her own. "Good for you!" she said warmly. "I like that smile! Keep it up!"

And that's just what I intended to do.

Hoping and Praying

I vividly recall the day that my best friend Chani's sister got engaged. Chani was glowing as she walked into the classroom that morning; she had turned into an instant celebrity.

"Mazel tov!" everyone screeched.

"You better have pictures!" someone demanded. "Otherwise, we are sending you home!"

Chani giggled as she pulled a digital camera out of her schoolbag.

"It wasn't official until late at night," she said, turning on her camera, "and then the *l'chaim* lasted until one o'clock in the morning! But I just had to come to school on time this morning to collect my mazel tovs!"

The others laughed as they gathered around Chani's

desk to admire the pictures and gush over the new *chassan* and *kallah*.

I glanced at a few of the pictures and then wished Chani mazel tov, too. Then I returned to my desk and slumped into my seat.

Thankfully, the others around me were too absorbed to notice my bad mood. I busied myself with my Chumash notes as I fought back my tears. *Don't cry,* I commanded myself. *Your best friend's sister just got engaged! You can't be in a bad mood!* But there was no denying to myself the pain that I was in.

Just then our teacher, Mrs. Bloch, walked into the room, and the huddle around Chani's desk quickly dispersed.

"I just heard the wonderful news," Mrs. Bloch said to Chani. "Mazel tov! So tell me, who's the *chassan*?"

I caught another glimpse of Chani's beaming face as she rattled off all the exciting details about the *shidduch*—the *chassan's* name, where he was from, where he learned—and I had to look away. Again, I had to control myself so that I wouldn't begin crying.

I'm not a bad person; I truly was happy for my friend. It was just that...well, Chani's sister, the *kallah*, was all of nineteen years old. And my own sister, Hindy, was twenty-eight years old...and still single.

Although I was much younger when Hindy came back from seminary, I couldn't wait for her to get engaged and married. I dreamed of parties, gowns, updos, and nieces and nephews. But the days—and then years—slowly passed...and we are still waiting for all that to happen...

While of course, the situation is hardest on my sister (and on my parents), it has also been very difficult for me. First of all, I worry constantly: when, oh, when, will the right one come around for Hindy? Will she *ever* get married? And if she has to wait for so many years to find her *bashert*, will the same thing happen to me? What if she hasn't gotten married by the time *I* come back from seminary and want to start *shidduchim*?

I know how counter-productive and harmful worrying is, but honestly, sometimes, I just can't help it.

Then, there is the heavy and gloomy atmosphere in my home. When one person in a family suffers, the rest of the family inevitably suffers as well. There are the anxious conversations from the other room that I know I am not supposed to hear and the countless phone calls to *shadchanim*. At times, I feel like my parents are so preoccupied with my older sister that they don't have any time for me!

There are also the raised hopes—the times when it seems like the right one has finally come, the times when I begin taking a survey of my closet, trying to decide what I should wear to the *vort*...and then, before I even reach a definite decision, the hopes come crashing down. No engagement, no *chassan*, and no *vort*. Just a whole lot of tears.

Then I am faced with a sticky dilemma: what am I supposed to say to my older sister when I see her crying bitterly after receiving disappointing news? I feel like I have to say *something* to her—I can't just ignore her pain—but hey, I'm only sixteen! What do I know about *shidduchim,* what's appropriate to say in such a situation and what isn't?

I also have to contend with my negative thoughts. Thoughts like: *Perhaps Hindy is being too picky and she's the one to blame for this whole miserable situation.* Or: *Maybe there is something wrong with our family and nobody wants us.* Or: *Are we not doing enough* hishtadlus, *and that's why this is happening?*

I have to work hard to fight these harmful thoughts and instead turn to my siddur and *daven* for my sister's *yeshuah.* Because, at the end of the day, that is the only productive thing I can do, the only thing that can bring some measure of comfort to my sister and hope to my parents.

Oh, how I wait for that day, when Hindy does get engaged, *b'ezras Hashem!* On that day, I know, the gray clouds hovering over my home will disappear, and my family will smile—*really* smile—and be able to rejoice fully in others' *simchos* once again...

In the meantime, though, I keep hoping and praying...

Honest with Myself

Raizy's compliment felt good. In fact, it felt very good.

"Nice shoes," she had commented lazily when I went to visit her one Friday night. She was sprawled out on her couch, magazine in hand.

"It was such a long week and I am utterly exhausted!" she declared as she stood up and gracefully slipped her feet into her slippers.

Visiting Raizy was always fun, a breath of fresh air. We always had so much to discuss, notes to compare, lives to contrast. Although we were close friends from camp and lived within a few blocks of each other, Raizy and I attended different high schools and therefore did not get to see each other often. When we did, it was a real treat.

"I'm actually looking for new Shabbos shoes my-self," Raizy said. "Maybe I'll look for a pair like yours. They're really cute."

I smiled. "Glad you like them," I replied breezily. *Glad* was an understatement; I was thrilled! The hours I had spent hunting for the perfect pair of shoes had paid off. True, my sister thought they were "hideous"; she obviously knew nothing about fashion and about what was currently "in." Raizy, on the other hand, was a fashion authority; she also had impeccable taste. She knew what was beautiful and in style and what was not.

"So, what's new with you?" asked Raizy.

"Midterms began this week," I told her.

"What's *wrong* with your school?" Raizy shook her head. "Every time I talk to you, there are tests, mid-terms, and finals going on! When do they actually have time to *teach* you anything?" She winked, and I tittered at her joke. Raizy was funny!

We chatted for another while, and I heard all about the goings-on in Raizy's life. At one point, I glanced down at my watch.

"Yikes! My father is for sure home from shul, and I bet they're all waiting for me!" I jumped up.

"Wait!" Raizy protested. "I've got to show you the pics from my brother's bar mitzvah first. It will only take a sec. Just hang on."

It was hard to say no to Raizy, so I sat, feeling jittery in my seat, waiting for her to return with the "pics." Of course I wanted to see them, but I was also appre-hensive about making my entire family wait for me in order to start the Shabbos meal.

Raizy's "sec" turned into fifteen minutes, and I arrived home to a very annoyed family.

"Where were you?" my younger brother burst out. "I'm starving!"

"Chavi, the family has been waiting for you for half an hour," my father said sternly.

"Where *were* you, anyway?" asked my older sister.

"At Raizy's house," I replied, feeling a blush creep up my cheeks.

Was that a disapproving glance from my mother? It was.

But I'm already in eleventh grade; for goodness's sake, I'm old enough to choose my own friends! I thought to myself indignantly. I liked Raizy. I enjoyed hanging out with her. And she really *was* a great girl. What did my mother have against her?

That night, I had a hard time falling asleep. I was thinking about my friendship with Raizy. She really was a fantastic girl. And I did enjoy hanging out with her. So what were the turbulent feelings about it now? I couldn't pinpoint what was making me feel so uncomfortable.

In the stillness of the night, with no other distractions, I was able to chew things over better. And I began to realize that Raizy brought out a certain side of me...a side that was a bit more lax. I acted a bit differently around her than with my other friends. My mind raced as I replayed certain topics that we had discussed earlier that evening...the words and phrases we had used...

The soft glow of the moonlight shone through my window and I was able to make out the time; the clock on my wall read 1:15. It was really getting late. I had to fall asleep already!

Listen, so she is a bit more easygoing and "chilled" than the rest of my friends, I finally declared to my conscience. *But that is a good thing; every girl needs some down time, right?*

Right!

Was it really a good thing? Time would tell.

I had met Raizy that summer, and as the year progressed, we spent more and more time together. I was generally the one who visited her (usually on Shabbos), but occasionally, Raizy popped over to my house, too. I always found myself floundering on those occasions, usually ushering Raizy straight into my bedroom.

I was awed at the confidence with which Raizy spoke to my parents and older sister; it was almost as though she was their equal, the age difference notwithstanding. Raizy was cool.

When I was frustrated by something a friend of mine had said, or an incident that had occurred in school, I would pick up the phone and call Raizy. Often, she was busy, but she would call me back later in the evening. Then, I'd sit huddled in my bedroom, confiding in Raizy and laughing and kvetching with her. And somehow, she'd always *get* it. Best of all, she'd respond by offering some witty advice or her own humorous take on the topic. That always made me feel a lot better.

See, it's a good thing I have Raizy as a friend! I'd tell my conscience. *She is always there for me, and she really gives good advice.*

But in moments of deep honesty, I'd realize that the

very fact that I had to justify this friendship was a bad sign. My close friends from high school—Leah, Dubby, Ruti, and Rivka—were great. I never had to justify my friendships with *them*. On the other hand, I began to notice that so many of my conversations with these friends were on the boring side, even juvenile, compared to my discussions with Raizy.

Sometimes, if I wasn't careful, my friends would catch these vibes.

"So, are you busy with Raizy tonight, or do you have a few minutes to spare for us?" they'd ask.

Ouch. That would sting. So I'd try to make plans with my school friends *and* Raizy—but it never worked. My friends didn't go for Raizy's "*shtick*," as they put it. And in any case, Raizy didn't quite go for them. I was therefore forced to shift my loyalties between my school friends and Raizy.

Months passed, and I continued to bond with Raizy, while doing my best to stay as close to my school friends as possible. There were a few sticky times (such as Shabbos afternoons), but I generally managed to wiggle my way out of trouble and keep everyone happy, precariously balancing each friendship.

My wakeup call came on a Motza'ei Shabbos.

Shortly after Havdalah, I received a phone call from Raizy. "Hey, Chavi, wanna come with me to City Café tonight? I can pick you up in an hour."

Did I want to drive with Raizy to City Café? Did I ever want to! My friends and I did not yet have our licenses (our school regulated that), but Raizy already had hers. To drive with Raizy around town—just me and her—would be absolutely thrilling. Aside from that, I was hungry and in the mood of a yummy pasta dish and milkshake from City Café. Actually, Raizy would never approve of that choice—so make that a Greek salad and diet Coke. Whatever. The point was that I was hungry, and I wanted to go out with Raizy.

The problem? My other friends were supposed to come over tonight to study for some little math test.

I vacillated between the idea of studying with my school friends or partying with Raizy. The decision wasn't a hard one to make.

I told Raizy I'd call her right back, hung up with her, and quickly called Dubby. "Hi, Dubby, I'm so sorry to cancel for tonight—but do you think everyone could come over tomorrow afternoon instead?" I asked.

"But we wanted to do something *tonight*," Dubby said. "And I was thinking that after we study, maybe we could bake pizza…"

Bake pizza? How nerdy! I suppressed a smirk. "I know, but something came up," I told her. "Can you do a huge favor for me and tell the others that it won't work for me tonight?"

After that conversation, I quickly called Raizy back and told her I'd love to come with her.

"I'm going to get dressed now; I'll be ready whenever you are," I said.

Raizy sounded pleased. "Great! I'll be there soon."

I ran to attack my closet, in search of the perfect outfit. Twenty minutes later, I was waiting at the front door, pocketbook in hand.

"Where are you going?" my mother asked me. "I needed you to babysit tonight!"

"Me? But I'm going out with Raizy!"

My mother frowned. "I am afraid it won't work," she said.

What happened next shocked me—and my family. I burst into tears. "But I just can't cancel on Raizy!" I cried.

"You know," my mother commented, "whenever Raizy comes into the picture, you are tense and nervous—totally not yourself."

Even as I tried desperately to protest to that, I realized, deep down, just how true my mother's words were.

Eventually, I did cancel my plans with Raizy. She wasn't happy, but said that she'd go out with some other friends instead. I tried to reschedule my night with my friends—there was no reason for them not to come over to study and bake pizza if I was babysitting at home anyway—but they had already made alternative plans. It didn't seem like they wanted to change anything to accommodate me.

So I stayed home that night and babysat my younger brothers, without any friends to keep me company. And when the boys fell asleep, I was left to ponder what had happened that evening. It was time to be honest with myself—brutally honest. And under the harsh light of that glaring honesty, I could see that all my constant justifications about my friendship with Raizy were just that: justifications and excuses.

It wasn't about her. Raizy was Raizy. It was about me—what *I* was like when I was together with Raizy. And I wasn't happy with what I was like at those times. I didn't like that side of me.

The question remained as to what I would do about the situation, from here and on.

And I knew the answer to that question. Breaking away from such a glittery friendship as the one I had with Raizy wouldn't be easy. But it was something that I wanted—and needed—to do.

The Whole Picture

Drama Try-Outs Today, During Lunch.
A cluster of girls huddled beside the sign posted on the hallway bulletin board, their tones rising in excitement. Who would make it into the school play this year? A flutter of hope ran through each girl. Perhaps *she* would get the coveted lead role!

I stood beside the sign, observing the scene. I didn't join the heated conversation; why, I didn't even join the dream of snagging the main part—or even any part—in the play.

It's not because I didn't *want* to be part of the play; I wanted to be a part of it more than anyone else did. But I could never act in a play, because I have trouble with my speech. You see, I stutter. And while I can generally get by on a day-to-day basis even with my impairment, my speech goes from bad to worse when I am put on the spot and have to talk in front of many people.

The thought of auditioning before the drama heads was scary. But to recite my lines on stage, in front of five hundred people or more? The thought of doing *that* was absolutely heart-stopping!

The day wore on, and lunch came and went, without me joining the masses of animated girls clustered outside the try-outs room. My friends returned after lunch, breathless yet exhilarated.

"The play sounds awesome this year!" announced Chany. All the others agreed with her.

"I hope I wasn't *too* dramatic when I tried out," Shaindy said.

Another animated discussion followed—and once again, I was left feeling out of things, all because of my stutter.

I often reflect on the way a slight stutter can cause such aggravation in a girl's life. In my case, due to my stutter, I often feel like I can't be who I want to be and I can't convey my true feelings and opinions.

See, teenage girls talk. A LOT. All the time. And they talk very quickly. If you want to squeeze your thoughts and opinions into a teen's conversation, you really have to be on your toes! I often have things to say, but it is unimaginably difficult and nerve-wracking for me to get the words out and in time.

Before talking, I have to really think about what I

want to say. It takes a tremendous amount of concentration and effort to get the words that are formulated in my head, out of my mouth. Certain sounds are harder for me to pronounce than others; for example, since I was little, I've had trouble with the "p" sound. To my embarrassment, I often just can't say it right!

I went to a speech therapist for years, and I did learn some techniques to help me overcome my stutter. But no technique could take my stutter away completely—unless you count the "whisper technique." If I whisper, then my stutter seems to magically disappear. Sounds good...but I can't spend my whole life whispering!

It may be difficult for girls who have never stuttered to comprehend the difficulties I face. Just how nerve-wracking is it for me? Let me answer that question by telling you about the following scenario: I was in seventh grade and my class was reading a literature story. My teacher came up with a system in which each girl would have a turn to read; we'd take turns by going up and down the rows of girls.

My class was engrossed in the captivating story. I, however, couldn't pay attention to anything but my pounding heart and my growing dread, as I mentally calculated the amount of girls ahead of me who had not yet received a turn to read.

Six more girls...five more girls... Another few pages into the story and we were down to two more girls. I shifted uncomfortably in my seat. I glanced at the door. I looked around the classroom. Each girl was sitting quietly, head bowed slightly, following along in her literature book.

One more girl... That meant my turn was next. Each

word the girl read aloud rang painfully in my ear, because it meant that my turn was one word closer. What would I do? There was no way in the world that I could read in front of my entire class. I just couldn't do it!

And then, at the last second, I came up with a plan. It wasn't a very wise plan, and it wasn't a long-term solution, but it worked: I made a great scene and dropped to the floor in a pretend faint. I was immediately sent to the nurse, my parents picked me up from school...and thankfully, I didn't have to read in front of my entire class.

That's how hard it was for me to read in front of other people with my stutter!

Again, I know it is hard to understand, but I often think that if a regular girl would stutter for even one complete day, she would "get it." It is not easy. (Thankfully, my speech has improved greatly over the years, and reading in public is no longer as frightening for me.)

So conversing is difficult for me; acting is impossible. Nonetheless, all of this is only a small part of the problem. What's hardest for me about my stutter is the way people perceive me because of my impairment.

Because I can't act in the school play, I am always put in choir. This is fine, really, because I have a nice voice and I don't stutter when I sing. I've even had solos, which always makes me feel great about myself. But some of the compliments that I receive from others after these solos can ruin my entire good feeling.

"Oh, it's *sooo* good that you sing, because your singing is totally fine, and now you can really be accepted into society," someone once commented to me.

Huh? Seriously? What was *that* supposed to mean? That until I came around and sang some songs, I *wasn't* part of society?

I wanted to tell the girl, *I am a completely regular person! My speech may be a bit different than yours, but that doesn't affect my IQ, my feelings, the way I treat other people, or the way I want to be treated and perceived by others!*

Or, take the comments I often get when meeting others for the first time and they don't know how to react to my speech impairment. On the first day of camp, a girl walked up to me with a, "Hi, what's your name?" But just then, my mouth seemed to freeze, and I just *couldn't* get my name out.

The girl waited a moment for me to respond before finally giving me a strange look. "What? You forgot your name?"

I knew she wasn't being intentionally nasty, but her words sure felt cruel to me.

Of course I didn't forget my name, I wanted to tell her. *It just doesn't roll off my tongue like it does for you and the rest of the world!*

Other times, when people hear me stutter, they'll quickly reassure me that, "Oh, I know someone else who stutters, too!" As if that will make me feel so much more comfortable stuttering to them.

Worst is when they talk to me like a baby: "Ohhh, don't *worry* about the stutter!"

Of course I'll worry about it if people treat me like this!

There are approximately sixty million people in the world who stutter, so I know I am definitely not alone in this. I felt compelled to share my thoughts, feelings, and experiences as a girl who stutters, because I want others to learn how to treat people like me.

Please, don't finish our words for us; don't tell us to slow down (trust me, that tidbit of advice doesn't help!). What *can* you do? Be patient. Don't change the subject of our conversation; just give us some time to finish our sentence. And please, look at the *real* person you're speaking to, not just her impairment.

My speech impairment does not generally affect my social standing, because once people make the effort to get to know me, they recognize who I *really* am. (And I don't mean to brag, but I am a cute and intelligent girl, full of spunk!) When I am with my good friends and people who make me feel comfortable, my speech is a lot better.

Due to my speech impairment, I have gained an extra sensitivity and patience for others, and for that I am grateful. I have learned to accept other people for who they are, even if they have challenges, because I know how much *I* have to offer and I surely wouldn't want anyone to get hooked onto a tiny—and relatively trivial—part of me. I want all of my friends and all those I meet to see the whole picture of who I am—the whole me!

True Connection

Sitting in the large auditorium for my high school's orientation, my pulse quickened as I fingered the handout I'd just received. Printed on it was my new high school schedule. I felt a sense of thrill; high school would be a totally new experience for me. Things would be so different than they had been in elementary school!

"Wow! There are too many teachers to count," I commented aloud. I smiled despite myself; at least that would bring some excitement and variety to my high school days. If I didn't particularly enjoy one teacher, I'd have plenty of others!

I slipped the schedule into a sheet protector and studied it carefully. My eyes drifted to the top of the paper. There, in bold letters, it read:

8:15-8:50: Tefillah

Now that was a lot to swallow. I mentally calculated the *davening* period—thirty-five minutes long—and began to wonder: *Does it really take each other girl in this school thirty-five minutes to* daven? Yes, I knew *davening* was important—but thirty-five minutes? That sure sounded like quite a long time to me!

I thought back to my short *davening* slots over the summer. I don't think it had ever taken me more than fifteen minutes to *daven* Shacharis, from start to finish. What in the world was I supposed to do with myself for an extra twenty minutes each morning?

"Uh, do they let you *daven* at home and then show up for first period at 8:55?" I asked some tenth graders who were sitting near me.

The girls began to giggle. Apparently, these seasoned tenth graders knew a whole lot more than I did.

"Nice try!" was the chirpy reply I received. "*Davening* in school is mandatory; they take attendance. Skipping it is like skipping first period!"

I nodded slowly. So much for that idea.

"Anyway," another girl spoke up, "*davening* in school is something that you wouldn't want to miss. The atmosphere in the *davening* room is a-*maaay*-zing. You'll see what I mean!"

Was she serious? I wondered. *Did she really enjoy* davening *in a room full of high school girls? For thirty-five minutes each morning?*

In preparation for my first morning of high school, I slipped my light pink siddur into my backpack. It was hard to ignore the intense emotions and persistent butterflies in my stomach as I walked to school. Would I make new friends? I fretted. Would I enjoy the classes? Would the workload overwhelm me? Would I like my teachers? And just as important—would they like me?

I was jittery and almost scared as I met my friends outside the school building at about 8:05. At least I had company with whom to walk inside the building. We nervous ninth graders meandered our way around—the clueless following the clueless—until we stumbled into the *davening* room just minutes before the bell rang.

I felt a tinge of relief. Being in such a nervous state was bound to help me *daven* well—I was pretty confident about that. The wonderful atmosphere in the *davening* room that I'd heard about would help me out, too, and surely I'd have the best *davening* in a long time!

When the bell rang, I settled into my seat, opened my siddur, and began with the *Birchos Hashachar*. I tried to focus and concentrate, but before I knew it, my mind was elsewhere. I was taking a mental survey of the shoes of the girls sitting around me. In between stanzas, I recognized quite a few pairs from my numerous trips to the mall. When I was bored of the shoes, I then studied hairstyles and jewelry...

Before I knew it, I was standing up for *Shemoneh Esrei*. Yikes! What had happened? I was supposed to have been mesmerized by the atmosphere in the room! I was supposed to have channeled my nerves into a heartfelt prayer to Hashem! Instead, I had busied myself with shoes and styles.

I lowered my head in shame. The worst part was that the girls around me had not even begun Shema yet! How embarrassing to be the quickest *davener* in the room! I busied myself for a few minutes until a safe number of others had begun *Shemoneh Esrei*; only then did I allow myself to start it, too. I wasn't about to broadcast my poor praying habits to the entire school!

When I finished *davening*, I sat down to wait. I glanced at my watch. Twelve more minutes to go. Again, I looked at the other girls *davening* around me. Some were swaying; others were standing in place with their *siddurim* covering their faces. I even noticed a girl who had tears in her eyes as she *davened*—and she didn't seem to be faking, either. I didn't get it. What did these girls know that I didn't?

Day after day, the *davening* sessions continued to be an immense struggle for me. I tried to focus, to concentrate, but my mind always seemed to wander away from the words leaving my mouth.

Months passed. I tried to listen attentively to the lessons we were taught about *tefillah*. I tried to internalize the messages. Each day, I'd gaze at some of the most sincere girls in the school as they *davened* and think to myself, *I wish I could be like them...* But despite all my efforts, the *davening* sessions continued to drag for me.

Of course, I never dared voice my true feelings; I just nodded along whenever my friends talked about the special *davening* room. In reality, though, I felt distant from the words in my siddur; I just couldn't connect.

Things continued in the same way even in tenth grade. My first day of tenth grade found me once again studying shoes in the *davening* room. *Oh, here I go again!* I thought to myself in frustration. Why was *davening* such a struggle for me? Why did these thirty-five minutes always pass by so slowly?

The turning point for me came in the middle of that year. Leah, my older sister, who had been "in *shidduchim*" for a few years already, joined me at the breakfast table one morning looking tired and pale.

"Are you okay?" I asked her.

She gave me a wan smile. "I had a hard night last night," she confessed to me. "You know, one of my last single friends just got engaged yesterday...and now I'm waiting for an answer from a *shadchan*... It's not easy..."

"Oh, I'm so sorry to hear that... I wish I could do something to make it easier for you..." My voice trailed off as I wracked my brain, trying to think how I could help Leah out. Her obvious pain broke my heart. "Can I make you a cup of coffee?" I finally offered.

She slowly shook her head. "I'd need a full barrel of coffee to get me through a day like today! But thanks anyway."

"Okay, then... *Hatzlachah rabbah!* Maybe you could try to take a nap before work or something..." I slung my schoolbag over my shoulder and made a beeline for the front door. I'm not really the "emotional type" and I was not particularly enjoying this conversation.

"Wait!" Leah called after me.

I paused and turned around.

"There *is* something you can do for me," she said. "You can *daven* for me."

"Uh... How big did you want that barrel of coffee to be?" I asked with a smile.

"No, really! I need you to *daven* for me, Devori," Leah said seriously.

Boy, talk about feeling uncomfortable! "Um...I guess...sure thing, I'll have you in mind," I hurriedly assured her before practically running outside.

That day, before reaching *Shemoneh Esrei*, I snapped to attention, recalling my promise to Leah. *I have to* daven *for her. I told her I would.*

I looked back into my siddur, and suddenly, the words seemed to take on new meaning. This was my beloved big sister Leah I was *davening* for! I so badly wanted her to have happiness...to find her *shidduch*... to begin building a family. Without my even realizing it, my eyes filled with tears. And I began to talk to Hashem.

I had no idea what was going on around me. I didn't know who had finished *davening* and who hadn't, who was swaying, who was crying, or who was wearing which shoes. I was too deep in conversation with Hashem. I was talking to Him, *really* talking to Him, telling Him about my sister's pain and asking Him to help her out.

I had never viewed *tefillah* as a personal connection, a real conversation, before. To me, it had always been a pressure, a chore, something that had to get done and crossed off the "to-do" list. But as I talked openly with Hashem that day, I finally understood what *davening* is all about.

Later that day, I found out that my sister's reply from the *shadchan* was a disappointing one. I knew that meant I had to continue *davening*, and I was determined to do just that—the right way.

Positive changes are never easy. These days, as much as I try to have conversations with Hashem like the one I had with Him back then, it doesn't always go. Sometimes, I still survey hairstyles, shoes, and necklaces during *davening*. But I do also have moments of intense connection. Once I tasted what true closeness with Hashem is all about, I discovered how wonderful it is and how much I want to continue having it.

And even when my family celebrated my sister's joyful engagement, when I was in eleventh grade, I continued to *daven* and talk to Hashem. Because I always need Him, and will always need Him—for the rest of my life.

Lights, Camera, Action

I had learned much about *ahavas Yisrael* from various teachers over the years, but what happened in my home this past Motza'ei Rosh Hashanah taught me the greatest lesson ever in *ahavas Yisrael*. It is truly a lesson I will never forget.

If you'd have passed by my house shortly after Rosh Hashanah, you would have been greeted by an astonishing sight: men, still dressed in their Yom Tov finery, were hustling about in the front yard, beneath massive bright lights that had been set up all along the lawn. You could almost see the question marks in our bewildered neighbors' eyes as they looked on at the odd scene, wondering what in the world was going on.

What was going on was a massive search for a missing ring. But let me give you some background to help you understand how and why this search had come about.

A few weeks before Rosh Hashanah, Rivka, a girl my sister knew from camp, contacted her. She had no place to spend Yom Tov, and she wanted to know if she would be able to spend it with my family. Rivka's story is heartbreaking. Her mother passed away when she was a young girl. She lived with her father, but he would be out of the country for Yom Tov.

My parents readily agreed to have Rivka over, and my family enjoyed a beautiful Yom Tov with her.

All was well until the ring incident. We were in the front yard, having just returned home from shul, when Rivka, deep in conversation with my sister, made a gesture with her hand that caused the ring she was wearing (which must have been a bit loose) to go flying.

To most of the world, that ring may have seemed like a simple piece of silver jewelry, but to Rivka, that ring represented a part of her mother; it was one of the few possessions she had from her. And now it was lost, buried somewhere in our yard.

Everyone immediately began scanning the yard for the ring, but as it was still Yom Tov, we couldn't do much. We made up to postpone the search until after Havdalah.

As soon as my father finished making Havdalah, we all hurried to the front yard and began a major search. My entire family got down on the ground, feeling around in the grass for the ring. We even dug up parts of the soil, just in case the ring had fallen into it and had been trampled upon. After a half hour of searching, we decided that we needed help (our front yard is quite large). What added to the pressure and anxiety was the fact that the landscapers were scheduled to come the next morning to do a large job on the yard.

My father pulled out his cell phone and called Chaveirim, a local organization that's dedicated to helping out fellow Jews in times of need.

"We have a slight emergency," my father said. "We lost an extremely valuable object. Do you think you can help us search for it?"

With no questions asked (other than our address), the Chaveirim dispatcher immediately sent out two volunteers to us. A few minutes later, they arrived and joined our search for the ring.

At one point, my father pulled the men aside and briefed them about the situation. He explained the sentimental value behind the ring.

"Well, in that case," said one of the men as he pulled out his cell phone, "this calls for backup."

Within a few minutes, Suburbans, cars, and emergency vehicles lined our block. The volunteers anxiously made their way to our yard; each one was given a small block of land to cover. Searchlights were set up, and shovels and yard tools given out. Before long, our yard was a hive of activity. Men swarmed across the expanse of the lawn, their eyes peeled to the ground. A couple of volunteers actually even climbed a tree, surmising that the ring could have landed up there when it flew off Rivka's finger.

The sight of so many people, all strangers to us and to Rivka, scurrying around the yard, desperately trying to help an orphaned teenage girl whose only connection to them was the fact that she was a fellow Yid, was a magnificent *kiddush Hashem*. It was a shining example of the unwavering unity of Klal Yisrael. The sight will always be embedded in my memory and in my heart.

The hours went by, and still the search continued in full force. But the missing ring, that tiny piece of jewelry that meant the world to Rivka, just could not be found. Finally, at 1:00 a.m., the volunteers decided to call it quits for the night. Slowly, they returned to their cars, and soon our front yard was once again quiet.

But one man refused to leave. He continued searching around until, a few minutes later, we heard a shout!

We all held our breaths as he bent down and picked something up... Yes! It was the ring! He had found it!

Someone ran inside to call Rivka. As soon as she came out, the volunteer handed the ring to her.

Rivka started crying; it was hard for her to talk. "Thank you," she managed. After a moment she asked him, "What is your name?"

"Chaveirim," he answered as he made his way back to his car.

Daughters of
the King

hat does Hashem want from me now?
Those were the words on the pins that our camp had given out to us before our major trip.

My friends and I were packed onto a bus, munching on nosh, singing off-key, harmonizing off-key, and chatting happily. Indeed, we were full of good spirits as we left on our much-anticipated trip to Hershey Park. Many of us had already been to Hershey Park before with our families, yet there is something exciting about boarding a bus and going somewhere with your camp friends. I was sure that this trip would be an entirely different experience than the one I had had with my family.

"Aliza, turn around and pose for a picture!" my friend Simi called to me.

I happily obliged. *Click.* We had already taken about twenty pictures and we hadn't even reached the highway yet!

Our bus finally merged onto the highway, and the soft breeze that drifted through the bus was refreshing. The words of our TC theme song rang through the bus.

I turned to my seatmate. "If I'd get a dollar for every time I heard that song this summer, I'd be a very rich girl!"

She shrugged; the singing had completely drowned out my words.

Oh, well. Loyal TC camper that I was, I quickly stopped trying to talk and instead joined in with the spirited singing.

We were in a bubble of our own, oblivious to the world around us. The bus driver could have driven us to the moon and we probably wouldn't have noticed! In fact, when he stalled at the side of the road, it took us a good few minutes to catch on.

I was actually the one who brought it to my friends' attention. "Hey, it looks like we broke down or something!"

My announcement was met with a series of shrieks and shrills. "Oh! My! Gosh!" exclaimed my seatmate as she glanced out the window.

"Young ladies!" the driver called out.

We quieted down at once, and he explained what was happening. Apparently, it was some kind of minor issue with the bus's engine, and he had called for back-up. He reassured us that it was just a matter of time until it would be fixed.

"But in the meantime," the bus driver said, "you should all get off the bus and wait in a nearby parking lot."

Oh, no. I groaned. What a waste of time! We were going to miss out on so much of the fun at Hershey Park!

For some reason, though, my friends were all excited by this adventurous turn of events. They grabbed their nosh bags—and cameras, of course—and skipped off the bus, thanking the driver and wishing him, "Good luck!" on the way.

I sighed and followed them, though inwardly I was grimacing with annoyance.

After we'd all waited in the hot sun for some time, one of my friends suggested that we walk over to a nearby supermarket to purchase some cold drinks. We obtained permission from our chaperones and made our way over to the store.

Lovely, we're going on a major trip to a supermarket, I thought cynically. *What fun!*

I was at the register, paying for my diet Coke. "I see that the store is swarming with charming young ladies in blue shirts," the cashier said to me with a smile.

I nodded. "We're all part of the same camp."

"Oh, are you?" said the cashier. "What a fine group you are! There are so many of you, but you are all so well-behaved!"

I smiled, glancing down at the pin on my shirt. "Our bus broke down outside," I explained to her. "We are waiting for them to fix it."

"Wow! And what positive attitudes you are all maintaining," she commented, as her pink nails clacked on the cash register.

I felt myself blush, thinking about the complaints and kvetches that were on the tip of my tongue.

We ended up waiting for two hours for the bus to be fixed. We amused ourselves by chatting, playing a few games, noshing, and of course, taking pictures.

When the driver finally called us back to the bus, we were only too happy to continue on our next leg of the journey.

After merging onto the highway again, the bus driver suddenly reached for his mike. "I want to tell you all something," he announced.

We quieted down, wondering what he was going to say.

"I've been a New York state trooper for fifteen years and then a bus driver for twenty years. I've seen quite a few mishaps and accidents in my days. And, I have to say, I've *never* seen a group of passengers react so well to a misadventure before. You all remained calm and patient; not one of you pestered me for an update every few minutes. I've never seen a group of kids like you."

Wow. That was our second compliment of the day. Perhaps this breakdown incident wasn't a waste of time, after all. It was a good thing I hadn't ruined this beautiful *kiddush Hashem* by sharing my gloomy thoughts with the others! I smiled as I watched a few of my friends glance at their pins.

We finally arrived at Hershey Park, and the fun began in earnest!

Hours later, we were standing in line for one of the rides, when a woman approached us. "Nice shirts!" she said. "This park seems to be full of girls who are wearing them. And I want to tell you that, in my opinion, you are the best-dressed people in this park—*and* the most well-behaved!"

My friends and I shared a warm smile. That was our third compliment of the day, and, boy, did it feel good!

Life is a test. It is not always easy to know exactly what Hashem wants from us. Yet, one thing is for certain: He always wants us to make a *kiddush Hashem*. And, reflecting on that camp trip to Hershey Park, I truly believe that my friends and I had acted like real daughters of the King. We had made a *kiddush Hashem*; we had made the King proud.

My Memorable Summer

It was late at night when I sat huddled on a bench in Camp Simcha, crying on the phone to my mother. "I don't know why I agreed to do this! I am going to have to work so crazy hard this summer...I don't think I'm cut out for this job."

Indeed, it seemed like I was in for a very difficult summer. I had just arrived at Camp Simcha and was waiting for my camper—a young woman with spina bifida (who was actually five years older than me)—to arrive. She was confined to a wheelchair, and my co-counselor and I had been told that we would have to tend to all of her physical needs—and I mean *all*. Aside from the activities in camp, we would have to shower, feed, and dress her. I had just sat through an intense session of training, and I was emotionally drained... and this was before my camper had even arrived!

"You can rise to the challenge—I know you can do it," my mother encouraged me. "And if things get difficult, just imagine what her parents have to go through. They deal with this on a regular basis, each and every day of the year. They never have a break from caring for their daughter, other than when she's away at camp."

That kind of put things into perspective. I was not in camp for myself. I was here to make someone else's life a little happier and a little easier. And, after all, it was only for two weeks. As my mother had said, my camper's parents did this *all year long*.

I walked back to my bunkhouse, thinking about my camper. I was here to give her a joyful summer, a respite from her usual life of doctors' appointments and hospitalizations. I looked at my camper's empty bed; tomorrow, she would be sleeping peacefully in it, secure in the knowledge that I would be taking care of her and giving her a great time...

And I will, I vowed to myself. *I'm going to give my camper the best summer possible.*

The next day, the campers' arrival day, dawned bright and clear. As I rushed around the bunkhouse, preparing to meet my camper, I had no idea that this would be a day I'd never, ever forget.

How can I describe the scene as the campers arrived? There was such a genuine sense of anticipation and excitement in the air...indeed, it seemed as though the very air was charged with electricity! All of the staff members got dressed up in hysterical, colorful costumes and stood at the camp entrance, eagerly awaiting the buses and cars that would be pulling up.

Amidst the tangible excitement, I watched as parents drove up to the camp grounds, their special-needs children in tow. Some of these campers were as young as five years old! It isn't hard to imagine how scary it must be for parents to hand over their special-needs child to someone else to take care of for two weeks. But as each set of parents let go of their child's hand, hundreds of staff members grabbed the camper and started dancing and singing with her. The parents of the children just stood back and cried.

These were children who, due to their limitations and disabilities, did not have many opportunities to have fun with friends. But enter Camp Simcha Special, and suddenly these same children had three hundred new friends (Camp Simcha Special's staff) who wanted nothing more than to hold their hands, dance with them, and give them the best time ever! Can there be a more beautiful sight than that?

The subsequent days passed in a blur of thrilling activities, shows and concerts, endless singing and dancing, and yes, a lot of difficult physical work. I had never worked so hard in my life. But when the last day of camp arrived, I found myself crying again—this time out of a sense of sadness and longing.

I was sad that camp was over. I had grown to love my camper, and caring for her had become a privilege I looked forward to each day. I would miss her terribly. I had spent my summer giving to another person—but in reality, I had gained so much more than I had given.

My summer taught me some magnificent lessons. I learned about how capable I really was. Yes, I worked very hard that summer, but I survived. And not only did I survive, but I left Camp Simcha Special a changed person—for the better. I'd spent so much time with such special *neshamos*, and in such a sublime and uplifting environment, I couldn't possibly be the same person I'd been before.

For that, I thank you, Camp Simcha Special.

Purim in the Psychiatric Hospital

When people think about uplifting Yom Tov experiences, they think of many things. But for me, right on top of the list is the Purim morning some friends and I spent doing *chessed* in a psychiatric hospital...

A few days before Purim, I was at my tutoring job, helping little Brochie Klein with her homework. After Brochie and I had finished, her mother walked me to the door. Something about the distraught expression on her face prompted me to ask, "Mrs. Klein, is everything okay?"

Mrs. Klein shook her head, her eyes glistening with tears. She went on to tell me about her older daughter, Yitty, who had to be in a psychiatric hospital for some time. As Purim was soon approaching, it looked like Yitty would be spending the festive day all by herself there. Mrs. Klein and her husband would visit her, of course, but as they had a house full of kids at home, they wouldn't be able to stay for too long.

"The idea of Yitty being alone in the hospital for the whole Purim is just so horrible," Mrs. Klein said, wiping her eyes, "but no one really knows that she's there, so it's not like we could expect her to get any other visitors..."

I made a split-second decision. Before I even had time to work out the technicalities in my head, I heard myself say, "Mrs. Klein, I'll visit your daughter on Purim. Really, I'd be happy to; I'll go with a friend or two, we'll bring her *mishloach manos*—we'll have a great time together!"

Mrs. Klein had no words to thank me; she was so incredibly grateful. I quickly jotted down the hospital's address, phone number, and pertinent information. Yes, Purim would be a busy day. But some things take precedence; somehow I would make this visit work out.

Purim morning, shortly after the *Megillah* reading, I picked up my friends Miri and Malka. With cups of coffee and muffins to fortify us, as well as a trunk full of *mishloach manos*—I had decided to bring along some extra *mishloach manos* packages in case we happened to meet up with any other Jewish children there—we set out for the psychiatric hospital.

We were just merging onto the highway when I casually mentioned to my friends that we would probably be searched when we arrived at the hospital. "It seems like that is the common practice when visiting the psychiatric hospital," I told them.

"The *what*?" asked Miri, shocked. "I thought we were going to the *Children's* Hospital!"

I giggled nervously. "Oh, we are—we're going to the *pediatric* psychiatric unit. Don't worry, it's totally going to be fine."

I just hoped I was right about that.

Upon arriving at the hospital, we walked down a long corridor and then came to a thick metal door. We were slightly apprehensive as we rang the bell. Would any of the patients attack us? And how would the hospital staff treat us?

A few minutes later, we were escorted inside by a nurse and led to the front desk. As we followed the nurse, balancing the bag of elaborate gift arrangements, we passed a large room where a group of noisy teenagers was watching a video.

We suddenly heard a voice call out, "A *freilichin* Purim!"

My friends and I exchanged glances. We scanned the crowd, trying to figure out who had shouted that greeting to us, but we couldn't figure out which kid it had been. In the meantime, we had to sign in at the front desk and present photo identification of ourselves. We were also searched, together with our *mishloach manos* packages. Some items that were classified as potentially hazardous material, such as the cellophane and ribbons, were confiscated.

"Okay, girls, you're good to go," the nurse said cheerfully to us.

I decided to ask the nurse about the Jewish kid who had wished us a *freilichin* Purim.

"Excuse me," I said politely, "but as we walked in,

one of the children over there"—I gestured to the large room from which blared the sounds of a video—"wished us a happy holiday. We actually brought some extra gift packages with us. I realize you can't share any identifying information with us, but is there any way you can tell us which one of the children in that room is Jewish? And is there any way we can give that child a holiday gift?"

"Oh, sure," answered the nurse. "His name is Ari; he is the one in the orange sweatshirt. And it is totally fine for you to give him a holiday gift. I actually think it will do a lot to cheer him up!"

On our way to Yitty's room, we made a detour. We walked over to the boy wearing the orange sweatshirt.

"Hi, Ari!" my friends and I greeted him. We wished him a hearty, "A *freilichen* Purim!" and gave him three different *mishloach manos* packages. They were missing their cellophane and carefully matched ribbons, but Ari's face lit up. We could tell that he thought the packages were beautiful.

"Hey, guys, thank you so much," he said simply.

My heart went out to him. I hadn't the foggiest idea of who this Ari was or why he was in a psychiatric hospital. One thing was clear, though: Watching a video in a dreary hospital is quite a miserable way for any Jewish child to spend Purim. Purim, after all, is supposed to be one of the happiest days of the year. It felt good to have been able to brighten Ari's day, even if only a bit.

The other children looked on enviously. "Today is a Jewish holiday," my friend Miri explained to them. "And Ari is a Jew—so we brought him a holiday gift."

We continued on to Yitty's room. After introducing

ourselves, we placed some *mishloach manos* packages on her night table, sat down with her, and had a mini Purim *seudah* right there in the hospital room. We turned on some Purim music, danced with her, and cheered her up. Through the closed door, I heard a few kids saying, "Gosh, I wish *I* was a Jew!"

About an hour later, it was time for us to leave. The head nurse took out a large key ring and escorted us to the metal door that leads to the exit of the hospital.

"Wow, I'm really impressed with you girls," she said. "That was such an incredible way to spend your holiday."

"Oh, it was our pleasure," we answered breezily. "We were so happy to do it."

She slowly opened the door, and we filed out. The door was about to slam shut behind us when I saw it: the nurse was wearing a *Magen Dovid* necklace around her neck. She was Jewish, too.

I looked down at the one remaining *mishloach manos* in my hands. I glanced back at the nurse's necklace. *Just do it*, I told myself, and with that, I handed the nurse that last *mishloach manos* package.

"And this one is for you!" I told her. "Happy Purim from all of us!"

The nurse had tears in her eyes as she accepted the package and thanked us. When the heavy metal door slammed shut behind us, I felt grateful for having had the opportunity to make a *kiddush Hashem*. And I felt grateful for having had such a meaningful and uplifting Purim.